AF568078

BECOME SUCCESSFUL RIGHT NOW

In the same series

Become Your Best Self Right Now

Make Your Life Extraordinary Right Now

{354}

BECOME SUCCESSFUL RIGHT NOW

A MASTERCLASS FROM THE

SUPERGURUS

ALEPH

ALEPH BOOK COMPANY
An independent publishing firm
promoted by ***Rupa Publications India***

First published in India in paperback in 2023
by Aleph Book Company
7/16 Ansari Road, Daryaganj
New Delhi 110 002

This edition published in 2023. The acknowledgements on p. 150 constitute an extension of the copyright page.

ISBN: 978-93-95853-67-5

1 3 5 7 9 10 8 6 4 2

Printed in India.

Contents

SECTION I
HOW TO BECOME SUCCESSFUL

SECTION II
HOW TO STAY SUCCESSFUL

SECTION III
SUCCESS AND WELL-BEING

SECTION I

HOW TO BECOME SUCCESSFUL

.1.

Dale Carnegie

How to Win Friends and Influence People

Dale Carnegie's best-known book has sold over 30 million copies worldwide and has been on bestseller lists in India in multiple editions for decades. In this lesson, he sheds light on the importance of seeing things from another's point of view.

~

A FORMULA THAT WILL WORK WONDERS FOR YOU

Remember that other people may be totally wrong. But they don't think so. Don't condemn them. Any fool can do that. Try to understand them. Only wise, tolerant, exceptional people even try to do that.

There is a reason why the other man thinks and acts as he does. Ferret out that reason—and you have the key to his actions, perhaps to his personality.

Try honestly to put yourself in his place.

If you say to yourself, 'How would I feel, how would I react if I were in his shoes?' you will save yourself time and irritation, for 'by becoming interested in the cause, we are less likely to dislike the effect.' And, in addition, you will sharply increase your skill in human relationships.

'Stop a minute,' says Kenneth M. Goode in his book *How to Turn People Into Gold*, 'stop a minute to contrast your keen interest in your own affairs with your mild concern about anything else. Realize then, that everybody else in the world feels exactly the same way! Then, along with Lincoln and Roosevelt, you will have grasped the only solid foundation for interpersonal relationships; namely, that success in dealing with people depends on a sympathetic grasp of the other persons' viewpoint.'

Sam Douglas of Hempstead, New York, used to tell his wife that she spent too much time working on their lawn, pulling weeds, fertilizing, cutting the grass twice a week when the lawn didn't look any better than it had when they moved into their home four years earlier. Naturally, she was distressed by his remarks, and each time he made such remarks the balance of the evening was ruined.

After taking our course, Mr Douglas realized how foolish he had been all those years. It never occurred to him that she enjoyed doing that work and she might really appreciate a compliment on her diligence.

One evening after dinner, his wife said she wanted to pull some weeds and invited him to keep her company. He first declined, but then thought better of it and went out after her and began to help her pull weeds. She was visibly pleased, and together they spent an hour in hard work and pleasant conversation.

After that he often helped her with the gardening and complimented her on how fine the lawn looked, what a fantastic job she was doing with a yard where the soil was like concrete. Result: a happier life for both because he had learned to look at things from her point of view—even if the subject was only weeds.

In his book *Getting Through to People*, Jesse S. Nirenberg commented: 'Cooperativeeness in conversation is achieved when you show that you consider the other person's ideas and feelings as important as your own. Starting your conversation by giving the other person the purpose or direction of your conversation, governing what you say by what you would want to hear if you were the listener, and accepting his or her viewpoint will encourage the listener to have an open mind to your ideas.'*

I have always enjoyed walking and riding in a park near my home. Like the Druids of ancient Gaul, I all but worship an oak tree, so I was distressed season after season to see the young trees and shrubs killed off by needless fires. These fires weren't caused by careless smokers. They were almost all caused by youngsters who went out to the park to go native and cook a frankfurter or an egg under the trees. Sometimes, these fires raged so fiercely that the fire department had to be called out to fight the conflagration.

There was a sign on the edge of the park saying that anyone who started a fire was liable to fine and imprisonment, but the sign stood in an unfrequented part of the park, and few of the culprits ever saw it. A mounted policeman was supposed to look after the park; but he didn't take his duties

---

*Jesse S. Nirenberg, *Getting Through to People*, Englewood Cliffs, N.J.: Prentice Hall, 1963, p. 31.

too seriously, and the fires continued to spread season after season. On one occasion, I rushed up to a policeman and told him about a fire spreading rapidly through the park and wanted him to notify the fire department, and he nonchalantly replied that it was none of his business because it wasn't in his precinct! I was desperate, so after that when I went riding, I acted as a self-appointed committee of one to protect the public domain. In the beginning, I am afraid I didn't even attempt to see the other people's point of view. When I saw a fire blazing under the trees, I was so unhappy about it, so eager to do the right thing, that I did the wrong thing. I would ride up to the boys, warn them that they could be jailed for starting a fire, order with a tone of authority that it be put out; and, if they refused, I would threaten to have them arrested. I was merely unloading my feelings without thinking of their point of view.

The result? They obeyed—obeyed sullenly and with resentment. After I rode on over the hill, they probably rebuilt the fire and longed to burn up the whole park.

With the passing of the years, I acquired a trifle more knowledge of human relations, a little more tact, a somewhat greater tendency to see things from the other person's standpoint. Then, instead of giving orders, I would ride up to a blazing fire and begin something like this:

'Having a good time, boys? What are you going to cook for supper? I loved to build fires myself when I was a boy—and I still love to. But you know they are very dangerous here in the park. I know you boys don't mean to do any harm, but other boys aren't so careful. They come along and see that you have built a fire; so they build one and don't put it out when they go home and it spreads among the dry leaves and kills the trees. We won't have any trees here at all if we aren't more careful, you could be put in jail for building this fire. But I don't want to be bossy and interfere with your pleasure. I like to see you enjoy yourselves; but won't you please rake all the leaves away from the fire right now—and you'll be careful to cover it with dirt, a lot of dirt, before you leave, won't you? And the next time you want to have some fun, won't you please build your fire over the hill there in the sandpit? It can't do any harm there.... Thanks so much, boys. Have a good time.'

What a difference that kind of talk made! It made the boys want to cooperate. No sullenness, no resentment. They hadn't been forced to obey orders. They had saved their faces. They felt better and I felt better because I had handled the situation with consideration for their point of view.

Seeing things through another person's eyes may ease tensions when personal problems become overwhelming. Elizabeth Novak of New South Wales, Australia, was six weeks late with her car payment. 'On a Friday,' she reported, 'I received a nasty phone call from the man who was handling my account informing me if I did not come up with $122 by Monday morning I could anticipate further action from the company. I had no way of raising the money over the weekend, so when I received his phone call first thing on Monday morning I expected the worst. Instead of becoming upset I looked at the situation from his point of view. I apologized most sincerely for causing him so much inconvenience and remarked that I must be his most troublesome customer as this was not the first time I was behind in my payments.

His tone of voice changed immediately, and he reassured me that I was far from being one of his really troublesome customers. He went on to tell me several examples of how rude his customers sometimes were, how they lied to him and often tried to avoid talking to him at all. I said nothing. I listened and let him pour out his troubles to me. Then, without any suggestion from me, he said it did not matter if I couldn't pay all the money immediately. It would be all right if I paid him $20 by the end of the month and made up the balance whenever it was convenient for me to do so.'

Tomorrow, before asking anyone to put out a fire or buy your product or contribute to your favorite charity, why not pause and close your eyes and try to think the whole thing through from another person's point of view? Ask yourself: 'Why should he or she want to do it?' True, this will take time, but it will avoid making enemies and will get better results—and with less friction and less shoe leather.

'I would rather walk the sidewalk in front of a person's office for two hours before an interview,' said Dean Donham of the Harvard Business School, 'than step into that office without a perfectly clear idea of what I was going to say and what that person—from my knowledge of his or her interests and motives—was likely to answer.'

That is so important that I am going to repeat it in italics for the sake of emphasis.

I would rather walk the sidewalk in front of a person's office for two hours before an interview than step into that office without a perfectly clear idea of what I was going to say and what that person—from my knowledge of his or her interests and motives—was likely to answer.

If, as a result of reading this book, you get only one thing—an increased tendency to think always in terms of the other person's point of view, and see things from that person's angle as well as your own—if you get only that one thing from this book, it may easily prove to be one of the stepping stones of your career.

.2.

Devdutt Pattanaik

The Success Sutra

Devdutt Pattanaik is a bestselling author and highly regarded speaker and interpreter of myth and religion. The author of dozens of books, he is especially celebrated for his insights into mythology and how these can be used in the fields of personal development, management, and governance. Here, he talks about balancing growth and stability.

~

If ambition is the force, then contentment is the counterforce

Growth drives most organizations. Along with growth comes change, and change is frightening. In the pursuit of growth, one must not lose sight of the stability of things already achieved.

The most common example of force and counterforce in mythology are the devas and asuras. The devas are not afraid of death but they are afraid of losing everything they possess. On the other hand, the asuras are afraid of death but have nothing to lose, as they possess nothing. This makes devas insecure and the asuras ambitious.

The devas want to maintain the status quo whereas the asuras are unhappy with the way things are. The devas want stability, the asuras want growth. The devas fear change and do not have an appetite for risk while the asuras crave change and have a great appetite for risk. The devas enjoy yagna, where agni transforms the world around them; the asuras practise tapasya where tapa transforms them, making them more skilled, more powerful, more capable. The devas enjoy Lakshmi, spend Lakshmi, which means they are wealth-distributors, but they cannot create her; the asuras are wealth-generators hence her 'fathers'. An organization needs both devas and asuras.

They need to form a churn, not play tug of war. In a churn, one party knows when to pull and when to let go. Each one dominates alternately. In a tug of war, both pull simultaneously until one dominates or until the organization breaks.

When Sandeep's factory was facing high attrition and severe market pressures, he ensured that old loyalists were put in senior positions. They were not particularly skilled at work. They were, in fact, yes-men and not go-getters, who yearned for stability. By placing them in senior positions, Sandeep made sure a sense of stability spread across the organization in volatile times. They were his devas who anchored the ship in rough seas. When things stabilized and the market started looking up, Sandeep hired ambitious and hungry people. These were asuras, wanting more and more. They were transactional and ambitious and full of drive and energy. Now the old managers hate the new managers and block them at every turn. Sandeep is upset. He wants the old guard to change, or get out of the way, but they will not change and refuse to budge. Sandeep is feeling exasperated and frustrated. He needs to appreciate the difference between devas and asuras. Each one has value at different times. They cannot combine well on the same team but are very good as force and counterforce during different phases of the organization. Sandeep must not expect either to change. All he needs to do is place them in positions where they can deliver their best.

If hindsight is the force, then foresight is the counterforce

Brihaspati is the guru of the cautious and insecure stability-seeking devas. Bhrigu-Shukra is the guru of the ambitious and focused, growth-seeking asuras. Sadly, neither do the devas listen to Brihaspti nor do the asuras listen to Shukra.

Watching Indra immersed in the pleasures of Swarga,

Brihaspati cautioned him about an imminent attack by the asuras. 'They always regroup and attack with renewed vigour. This has happened before, it will happen again. You must be ready,' said Brihaspati. Indra only chuckled, ignored his guru and continued to enjoy himself, drinking sura, watching the apsaras dance and listening to the gandharvas' music. This angered Brihaspati, who walked away in disgust. Shortly thereafter, Indra learned that the asuras had attacked Amravati, but he was too drunk to push them away.

After Bali, the asura-king, had driven Indra out of Swarga, and declared himself master of sky, the earth, and the nether regions, he distributed gifts freely, offering those who visited him anything they desired. Vaman, a young boy of short stature, asked for three paces of land. Shukra foresaw that Vaman was no ordinary boy, but Vishnu incarnate and this simple request for three paces of land was a trick. He begged Bali not to give the land to the boy, but Bali sneered; he felt his guru was being paranoid. As part of the ritual to grant the land, Bali had to pour water through the spout of a pot. Shukra reduced himself in size, entered the pot and blocked the spout, determined to save his king. When the water did not pour out, Vaman offered to dislodge the blockage in the spout with a blade of grass. This blade of grass transformed into a spear and pierced Shukra's eyes. He jumped out of the pot yelling in agony. The spout was cleared for the water to pour out and Vaman got his three paces of land. As soon as he was granted his request, Vaman turned into a giant: with two steps, he claimed Bali's entire kingdom. With the third step, he shoved Bali to the subterranean regions, where the asura belonged.

Brihaspati stands for hindsight and Shukra stands for foresight. Brihaspati is associated with the planet Jupiter, known in astrology for enhancing rationality, while Shukra is associated with the planet Venus, known for enhancing intuition. Brihaspati has two eyes and so, is very balanced. Shukra is one-eyed and so, rather imbalanced. Brihaspati is logical, cautious, and backward looking while Shukra is spontaneous, bold, and forward-thinking. Brihaspati relies on tradition and past history, or case studies. Shukra believes in futuristic creative visualization and scenario planning; his father Bhrigu is associated with the science of forecasting. Brihaspati relies on memory while Shukra prefers imagination. Both are needed for an organization to run smoothly.

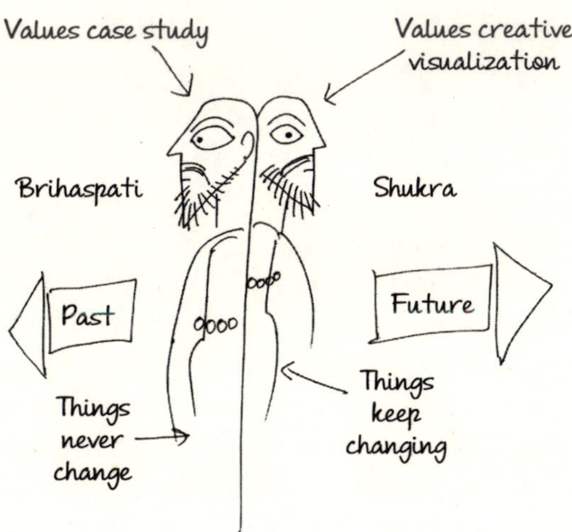

When Rajiv was presenting his vision and business plan to his investors, he realized they were making fun of him.

His ideas seemed too strange and bizarre. They said, 'Give us proof of your concept.' And, 'Tell us exactly how much the return on investment will be.' Rajiv tried his best to answer these questions, but his idea was radical and had never been attempted before. It was a new product, like the iPad had been at its inception. He would have to create a market for it. He had sensed people's need for it though this need was not explicit. It was a hidden need, waiting to be tapped. Rajiv is a Shukra—he can see what no one else has yet seen. The investors before him are Brihaspati—they trust only what has already been seen.

.3.

Napoleon Hill

Think and Grow Rich

Napoleon Hill's Think and Grow Rich *is one of the most popular self-help books of all time and has sold tens of millions of copies since it was first published in 1937–sales estimates range from a low of 20 million copies to over 70 million copies. In this extract, Napoleon Hill provides tips on leadership.*

~

THE MAJOR ATTRIBUTES OF LEADERSHIP

The following are important factors of leadership:

1. UNWAVERING COURAGE based upon knowledge of self, and of one's occupation. No follower wishes to be dominated by a leader who lacks self-confidence and courage. No intelligent follower will be dominated by such a leader very long.
2. SELF-CONTROL. The man who cannot control himself, can never control others. Self-control sets a mighty example for one's followers, which the more intelligent will emulate.

3. A KEEN SENSE OF JUSTICE. Without a sense of fairness and justice, no leader can command and retain the respect of his followers.
4. DEFINITENESS OF DECISION. The man who wavers in his decisions, shows that he is not sure of himself. He cannot lead others successfully.
5. DEFINITENESS OF PLANS. The successful leader must plan his work, and work his plan. A leader who moves by guesswork, without practical, definite plans, is comparable to a ship without a rudder. Sooner or later he will land on the rocks.
6. THE HABIT OF DOING MORE THAN PAID FOR. One of the penalties of leadership is the necessity of willingness, upon the part of the leader, to do more than he requires of his followers.
7. A PLEASING PERSONALITY. No slovenly, careless person can become a successful leader. Leadership calls for respect. Followers will not respect a leader who does not grade high on all of the factors of a Pleasing Personality.
8. SYMPATHY AND UNDERSTANDING. The successful leader must be in sympathy with his followers. Moreover, he must understand them and their problems.
9. MASTERY OF DETAIL. Successful leadership calls for mastery of details of the leader's position.
10. WILLINGNESS TO ASSUME FULL RESPONSIBILITY. The successful leader must be willing to assume responsibility for the mistakes and the shortcomings of his followers. If he tries to shift this responsibility, he will not remain the leader. If one of his followers makes a mistake, and shows himself

incompetent, the leader must consider that it is he who failed.

11. COOPERATION. The successful leader must understand, and apply the principle of cooperative effort and be able to induce his followers to do the same. Leadership calls for POWER, and power calls for COOPERATION.

There are two forms of Leadership. The first, and by far the most effective, is LEADERSHIP BY CONSENT of, and with the sympathy of the followers. The second is LEADERSHIP BY FORCE, without the consent and sympathy of the followers.

History is filled with evidences that Leadership by Force cannot endure. The downfall and disappearance of Dictators and Kings is significant. It means that people will not follow forced leadership indefinitely.

The world has just entered a new era of relationship between leaders and followers, which very clearly calls for new leaders, and a new brand of leadership in business and industry. Those who belong to the old school of leadership-by-force, must acquire an understanding of the new brand of leadership (cooperation) or be relegated to the rank and file of the followers. There is no other way out for them.

The relationship of employer and employee, or of leader and follower, in the future, will be one of mutual cooperation, based upon an equitable division of the profits of business. In the future, the relationship of employer and employee will be more like a partnership than it has been in the past. Napoleon, Kaiser Wilhelm of Germany, the Czar of Russia, and the King of Spain were examples of leadership by force. Their leadership passed. Without much difficulty, one might point to the prototypes of these ex-leaders, among the business, financial, and labor leaders of America who have been dethroned or slated to go. Leadership-by-consent of the followers is the only brand which can endure!

Men may follow the forced leadership temporarily, but they will not do so willingly.

The new brand of LEADERSHIP will embrace the eleven factors of leadership, described in this chapter, as well as some other factors. The man who makes these the basis of his leadership will find abundant opportunity to lead in any walk of life. The depression was prolonged, largely, because the world lacked LEADERSHIP of the new brand. At the end of the depression, the demand for leaders who are competent to apply the new methods of leadership has greatly exceeded the supply. Some of the old type of leaders will reform and adapt themselves to the new brand of leadership, but generally speaking, the world will have to look for new timber for its leadership. This necessity may be your OPPORTUNITY!

THE 10 MAJOR CAUSES OF FAILURE IN LEADERSHIP

We come now to the major faults of leaders who fail, because it is just as essential to know WHAT NOT TO DO as it is to know what to do.

1. INABILITY TO ORGANIZE DETAILS. Efficient leadership calls for ability to organize and to master

details. No genuine leader is ever 'too busy' to do anything which may be required of him in his capacity as leader. When a man, whether he is a leader or follower, admits that he is 'too busy' to change his plans, or to give attention to any emergency, he admits his inefficiency. The successful leader must be the master of all details connected with his position. That means, of course, that he must acquire the habit of relegating details to capable lieutenants.

2. UNWILLINGNESS TO RENDER HUMBLE SERVICE.

   Truly great leaders are willing, when occasion demands, to perform any sort of labor which they would ask another to perform. 'The greatest among ye shall be the servant of all' is a truth which all able leaders observe and respect.

3. EXPECTATION OF PAY FOR WHAT THEY KNOW INSTEAD OF WHAT THEY DO WITH THAT WHICH THEY KNOW. The world does not pay men for that which they know. It pays them for what they DO, or induce others to do.

4. FEAR OF COMPETITION FROM FOLLOWERS.

   The leader who fears that one of his followers may take his position is practically sure to realize that fear sooner or later. The able leader trains understudies to whom he may delegate, at will, any of the details of his position. Only in this way may a leader multiply himself and prepare himself to be at many places, and give attention to many things at one time. It is an etemal truth that men receive more pay for their ABILITY TO GET OTHERS TO

PERFORM, than they could possibly earn by their own efforts. An efficient leader may, through his knowledge of his job and the magnetism of his personality, greatly increase the efficiency of others, and induce them to render more service and better service than they could render without his aid.

5. LACK OF IMAGINATION. Without imagination, the leader is incapable of meeting emergencies, and of creating plans by which to guide his followers efficiently.
6. SELFISHNESS. The leader who claims all the honor for the work of his followers, is sure to be met by resentment. The really great leader CLAIMS NONE OF THE HONORS. He is contented to see the honors, when there are any, go to his followers, because he knows that most men will work harder for commendation and recognition than they will for money alone.
7. INTEMPERANCE. Followers do not respect an intemperate leader. Moreover, intemperance in any of its various forms destroys the endurance and the vitality of all who indulge in it.
8. DISLOYALTY. Perhaps this should have come at the head of the list. The leader who is not loyal to his trust, and to his associates, those above him, and those below him, cannot long maintain his leadership. Disloyalty marks one as being less than the dust of the earth, and brings down on one's head the contempt he deserves. Lack of loyalty is one of the major causes of failure in every walk of life.
9. EMPHASIS OF THE 'AUTHORITY' OF LEADERSHIP. The efficient leader leads by encouraging,

and not by trying to instil fear in the hearts of his followers. The leader who tries to impress his followers with his 'authority' comes within the category of leadership through FORCE. If a leader is a REAL LEADER, he will have no need to advertise that fact except by his conduct—his sympathy, understanding, fairness, and a demonstration that he knows his job.

10. EMPHASIS OF TITLE. The competent leader requires no 'title' to give him the respect of his followers. The man who makes too much over his title generally has little else to emphasize. The doors to the office of the real leader are open to all who wish to enter, and his working quarters are free from formality or ostentation.

These are among the more common of the causes of failure in leadership. Any one of these faults is sufficient to induce failure. Study the list carefully if you aspire to leadership, and make sure that you are free of these faults.

.4.

Paramhansa Yogananda

Autobiography of a Yogi

Autobiography of a Yogi by Paramhansa Yogananda is one of the most important spiritual books of our time and has influenced people in every corner of the globe, including entrepreneurs like Steve Jobs of Apple and celebrities from the world of entertainment such as Ravi Shankar, George Harrison, Elvis Presley, Mariel Hemingway, and Dennis Weaver. Since its first publication in 1946, it has been translated into over 50 languages. In this extract, Paramhansa Yogananda relates the fascinating story of the Tiger Swami who exemplifies that power lies in will, confidence, and courage.

~

The Tiger Swami

'I have discovered the Tiger Swami's address. Let us visit him tomorrow.'

This welcome suggestion came from Chandi, one of my high school friends. I was eager to meet the saint who, in his premonastic life, had caught and fought tigers with his naked hands. A boyish enthusiasm over such remarkable feats was strong within me.

The next day dawned wintry cold, but Chandi and I sallied forth gaily. After much vain hunting in Bhowanipur, outside Calcutta, we arrived at the right house. The door held two iron rings, which I sounded piercingly. Notwithstanding the clamour, a servant approached with leisurely gait. His ironical smile implied that visitors, despite their noise, were powerless to disturb the calmness of a saint's home.

Feeling the silent rebuke, my companion and I were thankful to be invited into the parlour. Our long wait there caused uncomfortable misgivings. India's unwritten law for the truth seeker is patience; a master may purposely make a test of one's eagerness to meet him. This psychological ruse is freely employed in the West by doctors and dentists!

Finally summoned by the servant, Chandi and I entered a sleeping apartment. The famous Sohong* Swami was seated on his bed. The sight of his tremendous body affected us strangely. With bulging eyes, we stood speechless. We had never before seen such a chest or such football-like biceps. On an immense neck, the swami's fierce yet calm face was adorned with flowing locks, beard, and moustache. A hint of dovelike and tigerlike qualities shone in his dark eyes. He was unclothed, save for a tiger skin about his muscular waist.

Finding our voices, my friend and I greeted the monk, expressing our admiration for his prowess in the extraordinary feline arena.

'Will you not tell us, please, how it is possible to subdue

---

*Sohong was his monastic name. He was popularly known as the 'Tiger Swami.'

with bare fists the most ferocious of jungle beasts, the royal Bengals?'

'My sons, it is nothing to me to fight tigers. I could do it today if necessary.' He gave a childlike laugh. 'You look upon tigers as tigers; I know them as pussycats.'

'Swamiji, I think I could impress my subconsciousness with the thought that tigers are pussycats, but could I make tigers believe it?'

'Of course strength also is necessary! One cannot expect victory from a baby who imagines a tiger to be a house cat! Powerful hands are my sufficient weapon.'

He asked us to follow him to the patio, where he struck the edge of a wall. A brick crashed to the floor; the sky peered boldly through the gaping lost tooth of the wall. I fairly staggered in astonishment; he who can remove mortared bricks from a solid wall with one blow, I thought, must surely be able to displace the teeth of tigers!

'A number of men have physical power such as mine, but still lack in cool confidence. Those who are bodily but not mentally stalwart may find themselves fainting at mere sight of a wild beast bounding freely in the jungle. The tiger in its natural ferocity and habitat is vastly different from the opium-fed circus animal!

'Many a man with herculean strength has nonetheless been terrorized into abject helplessness before the onslaught of a royal Bengal. Thus the tiger has converted the man, in his own mind, to a state as nerveless as the pussycat's. It is possible for a man, owning a fairly strong body and an immensely strong determination, to turn the tables on the tiger, and force it to a conviction of pussycat defenselessness.

How often I have done just that!'

I was quite willing to believe that the titan before me was able to perform the tiger-pussycat metamorphosis. He seemed in a didactic mood; Chandi and I listened respectfully.

'Mind is the wielder of muscles. The force of a hammer blow depends on the energy applied; the power expressed by a man's bodily instrument depends on his aggressive will and courage. The body is literally manufactured and sustained by mind. Through pressure of instincts from past lives, strengths or weaknesses percolate gradually into human consciousness. They express as habits, which in turn ossify into a desirable or an undesirable body. Outward frailty has mental origin; in a vicious circle, the habit-bound body thwarts the mind. If the master allows himself to be commanded by a servant, the latter becomes autocratic; the mind is similarly enslaved by submitting to bodily dictation.'

At our entreaty, the impressive swami consented to tell us something of his own life.

'My earliest ambition was to fight tigers. My will was mighty, but my body was feeble.'

An ejaculation of surprise broke from me. It appeared incredible that this man, now 'with Atlantean shoulders, fit to bear,' could ever have known weakness.

'It was by indomitable persistency in thoughts of health and strength that I overcame my handicap. I have every reason to extol the compelling mental vigour which I found to be the real subduer of royal Bengals.'

'Do you think, revered swami, that I could ever fight tigers?'

This was the first, and the last, time that the bizarre ambition ever visited my mind!

'Yes.' He was smiling. 'But there are many kinds of tigers; some roam in jungles of human desires. No spiritual benefit accrues by knocking beasts unconscious. Rather be the victor over the inner prowlers.'

'May we hear, sir, how you changed from a tamer of wild tigers to a tamer of wild passions?'

The Tiger Swami fell into silence. Remoteness came into his gaze, summoning visions of bygone years. I discerned his slight mental struggle to decide whether to grant my request. Finally he smiled in acquiescence.

'When my fame reached a zenith, it brought the intoxication of pride. I decided not only to fight tigers but to display them in various tricks. My ambition was to force savage beasts to behave like domesticated ones. I began to perform my feats publicly, with gratifying success.

'One evening my father entered my room in a pensive mood.

'Son, I have words of warning. It would save you from coming ills, produced by the grinding wheels of cause and effect.'

'Are you a fatalist, Father? Should superstition be allowed to discolour the powerful waters or my activities?'

'I am no fatalist, son. But I believe in the just law of retribution, as taught in the holy scriptures. There is resentment against you in the jungle family; sometime it may act to your cost.'

'Father, you astonish me! You well know what tigers are—beautiful but merciless! Even immediately after an enormous meal of some hapless creature, a tiger is fired with fresh lust at sight of new prey. It may be a joyous gazelle, frisking over the jungle grass. Capturing it and biting an opening in the soft throat, the malevolent beast tastes only a little of the mutely crying blood, and goes its wanton way.

'Tigers are the most contemptible of the jungle breed! Who knows? My blows may inject some slight sanity of consideration into their thick heads. I am headmaster in a forest finishing school, to teach them gentle manners!

'Please, Father, think of me as a tiger tamer and never as a tiger killer. How could my good actions bring ill upon me? I beg you not to impose any command that will change my way of life.'

Chandi and I were all attention, understanding the past dilemma. In India a child does not lightly disobey his parents' wishes.

'In stoic silence Father listened to my explanation. He followed it with a disclosure which he uttered gravely.

'Son, you compel me to relate an ominous prediction from the lips of a saint. He approached me yesterday as I sat on the veranda in my daily meditation.

"Dear friend, I come with a message for your belligerent son. Let him cease his savage activities. Otherwise, his next tiger encounter shall result in severe wounds, followed by six months of deathly sickness. He shall then forsake his former ways and become a monk."'

'This tale did not impress me. I considered that Father had been the credulous victim of a deluded fanatic.'

The Tiger Swami made this confession with an impatient gesture, as though at some stupidity. Grimly silent for a long time, he seemed oblivious of our presence. When he took up the dangling thread of his narrative, it was suddenly, with subdued voice.

'Not long after Father's warning, I visited the capital city of Cooch Behar. The picturesque territory was new to me, and I expected a restful change. As usual everywhere, a curious crowd followed me on the streets. I would catch bits of whispered comment:

> 'This is the man who fights wild tigers.'
>
> 'Has he legs, or tree-trunks?'
>
> 'Look at his face! He must be an incarnation of the king of tigers himself!'

'You know how village urchins function like final editions of a newspaper! With what speed do the even-later speech-bulletins of the women circulate from house to house! Within a few hours, the whole city was in a state of excitement over my presence.

'I was relaxing quietly in the evening, when I heard the hoofbeats of galloping horses. They stopped in front of my dwelling place. In came a number of tall, turbaned policemen.

'I was taken aback. "All things are possible unto these creatures of human law," I thought. "I wonder if they are going to take me to task about matters utterly unknown to me."' But the officers bowed with unwonted courtesy.

'Honoured Sir, we are sent to welcome you on behalf of the Prince of Cooch Behar. He is pleased to invite you to his palace tomorrow morning.'

'I speculated awhile on the prospect. For some obscure reason I felt sharp regret at this interruption in my quiet trip. But the suppliant manner of the policemen moved me; I agreed to go.

'I was bewildered the next day to be obsequiously escorted from my door into a magnificent coach drawn by four horses. A servant held an ornate umbrella to protect me from the scorching sunlight. I enjoyed the pleasant ride through the city and its woodland outskirts. The royal scion himself was at the palace door to welcome me. He proffered his own gold-brocaded seat, smilingly placing himself in a chair of simpler design.

'All this politeness is certainly going to cost me something!' I thought in mounting astonishment. The prince's motive emerged after a few casual remarks.

'My city is filled with the rumour that you can fight wild tigers with nothing more than your naked hands. Is it a fact?'

'It is quite true.'

'I can scarcely believe it! You are a Calcutta Bengali, nurtured on the white rice of city folk. Be frank, please; have you not been fighting only spineless, opium-fed animals?' His voice was loud and sarcastic, tinged with provincial accent.

'I vouchsafed no reply to his insulting question.

"I challenge you to fight my newly caught tiger, Raja Begum.* If you can successfully resist him, bind him with a chain, and leave his cage in a conscious state, you shall have this royal Bengal! Several thousand rupees and many other gifts shall also be bestowed. If you refuse to meet him

---

*'Prince Princess'—so named to indicate that this beast possessed the combined ferocity of tiger and tigress.

in combat, I shall blazon your name throughout the state as an impostor!"

'His insolent words struck me like a volley of bullets. I shot an angry acceptance. Half risen from the chair in his excitement, the prince sank back with a sadistic smile. I was reminded of the Roman emperors who delighted in setting Christians in bestial arenas.

"The match will be set for a week hence. I regret that I cannot give you permission to view the tiger in advance."

'Whether the prince feared I might seek to hypnotize the beast, or secretly feed him opium, I know not!

'I left the palace, noting with amusement that the royal umbrella and panoplied coach were now missing.

'The following week I methodically prepared my mind and body for the coming ordeal. Through my servant I learned of fantastic tales. The saint's direful prediction to my father had somehow got abroad, enlarging as it ran. Many simple villagers believed that an evil spirit, cursed by the gods, had reincarnated as a tiger which took various demoniac forms at night, but remained a striped animal during the day. This demon-tiger was supposed to be the one sent to humble me.

'Another imaginative version was that animal prayers to Tiger Heaven had achieved a response in the shape of Raja Begum. He was to be the instrument to punish me—the audacious biped, so insulting to the entire tiger species! A furless, fangless man daring to challenge a claw-armed, sturdy-limbed tiger! The concentrated venom of all humiliated tigers—the villagers declared—had gathered momentum sufficient to operate hidden laws and bring about the fall of the proud tiger tamer.

'My servant further apprized me that the prince was in his element as manager of the bout between man and beast. He had supervised the erection of a storm-proof pavilion, designed to accommodate thousands. Its center held Raja Begum in an enormous iron cage, surrounded by an outer safety room. The captive emitted a ceaseless series of blood-curdling roars. He was fed sparingly, to kindle a wrathful appetite. Perhaps the prince expected me to be the meal of reward!

'Crowds from the city and suburbs bought tickets eagerly in response to the beat of drums announcing the unique contest. The day of battle saw hundreds turned away for lack of seats. Many men broke through the tent openings, or crowded any space below the galleries.'

As the Tiger Swami's story approached a climax, my excitement mounted with it; Chandi also was raptly mute.

'Amidst piercing sound explosions from Raja Begum, and the hubbub of the somewhat terrified crowd, I quietly made my appearance. Scantily clad around the waist, I was otherwise unprotected by clothing. I opened the bolt on the door of the safety room and calmly locked it behind me. The tiger sensed blood. Leaping with a thunderous crash on his bars, he sent forth a fearsome welcome. The audience was hushed with pitiful fear; I seemed a meek lamb before the raging beast.

'In a trice I was within the cage; but as I slammed the door, Raja Begum was headlong upon me. My right hand was desperately torn. Human blood, the greatest treat a tiger can know, fell in appalling streams. The prophecy of the saint seemed about to be fulfilled.

'I rallied instantly from the shock of the first serious injury I had ever received. Banishing the sight of my gory fingers by thrusting them beneath my waist cloth, I swung my left arm in a bone-cracking blow. The beast reeled back, swirled around the rear of the cage, and sprang forward convulsively. My famous fistic punishment rained on his head.

'But Raja Begum's taste of blood had acted like the maddening first sip of wine to a dipsomaniac long-deprived. Punctuated by deafening roar, the brute's assaults grew in fury. My inadequate defense of only one hand left me vulnerable before claws and fangs. But I dealt out dazing retribution. Mutually ensanguined, we struggled as to the death. The cage was pandemonium, as blood splashed in all directions, and blasts of pain and lethal lust came from the bestial throat.

"Shoot him!" "Kill the tiger!" Shrieks arose from the audience. So fast did man and beast move, that a guard's bullet went amiss. I mustered all my will force, bellowed fiercely, and landed a final concussive blow. The tiger collapsed and lay quietly.'

'Like a pussycat!' I interjected.

The swami laughed in hearty appreciation, then continued the engrossing tale.

'Raja Begum was vanquished at last. His royal pride was further humbled: with my lacerated hands, I audaciously forced open his jaws. For a dramatic moment, I held my head within the yawning deathtrap. I looked around for a chain. Pulling one from a pile on the floor, I bound the tiger by his neck to the cage bars. In triumph I moved toward the door.

'But that fiend incarnate, Raja Begum, had stamina

worthy of his supposed demoniac origin. With an incredible lunge, he snapped the chain and leaped on my back. My shoulder fast in his jaws, I fell violently. But in a trice I had him pinned beneath me. Under merciless blows, the treacherous animal sank into semiconsciousness. This time I secured him more carefully. Slowly I left the cage.

'I found myself in a new uproar, this time one of delight. The crowd's cheer broke as though from a single gigantic throat. Disastrously mauled, I had yet fulfilled the three conditions of the fight—stunning the tiger, binding him with a chain, and leaving him without requiring assistance for myself. In addition, I had so drastically injured and frightened the aggressive beast that he had been content to overlook the opportune prize of my head in his mouth!

'After my wounds were treated, I was honoured and garlanded; hundreds of gold pieces showered at my feet. The whole city entered a holiday period. Endless discussions were heard on all sides about my victory over one of the largest and most savage tigers ever seen. Raja Begum was presented to me, as promised, but I felt no elation. A spiritual change had entered my heart. It seemed that with my final exit from the cage I had also closed the door on my worldly ambitions.

'A woeful period followed. For six months I lay near death from blood poisoning. As soon as I was well enough to leave Cooch Behar, I returned to my native town.

'I know now that my teacher is the holy man who gave the wise warning.' I humbly made this confession to my father. 'Oh, if I could only find him!' My longing was sincere, for one day the saint arrived unheralded.

'Enough of tiger taming.' He spoke with calm assurance.

'Come with me; I will teach you to subdue the beasts of ignorance roaming in jungles of the human mind. You are used to an audience: let it be a galaxy of angels, entertained by your thrilling mastery of yoga!'

'I was initiated into the spiritual path by my saintly guru. He opened my soul-doors, rusty and resistant with long disuse. Hand in hand, we soon set out for my training in the Himalayas.'

Chandi and I bowed at the swami's feet, grateful for his vivid outline of a life truly cyclonic. I felt amply repaid for the long probationary wait in the cold parlour!

.5.

James Allen

As a Man Thinketh

James Allen, a British writer and thinker, wrote several inspirational and self-help books, the best-known of which is As a Man Thinketh. *It has touched the lives of millions since it was first published in 1903. Here, the author teaches us that well-directed thought leads to achievement.*

~

THOUGHT AND PURPOSE

Until thought is linked with purpose there is no intelligent accomplishment. With the majority the bark of thought is allowed to 'drift' upon the ocean of life. Aimlessness is a vice, and such drifting must not continue for him who would steer clear of catastrophe and destruction. They who have no central purpose in their life fall an easy prey to petty worries, fears, troubles, and self-pityings, all of which are indications of weakness, which lead, just as surely as deliberately planned sins (though by a different route), to failure, unhappiness, and loss, for weakness cannot persist in a power evolving universe.

A man should conceive of a legitimate purpose in his heart, and set out to accomplish it. He should make this purpose the centralizing point of his thoughts. It may take the form of a spiritual ideal, or it may be a worldly object, according to his nature at the time being; but whichever it is, he should steadily focus his thought-forces upon the object, which he has set before him. He should make this purpose his supreme duty, and should devote himself to its attainment, not allowing his thoughts to wander away into ephemeral fancies, longings, and imaginings. This is the royal road to self-control and true concentration of thought. Even if he fails again and again to accomplish his purpose (as he necessarily must until weakness is overcome), the strength of character gained will be the measure of his true success, and this will form a new starting-point for future power and triumph.

Those who are not prepared for the apprehension of a great purpose should fix the thoughts upon the faultless performance of their duty, no matter how insignificant their task may appear. Only in this way can the thoughts be gathered and focussed, and resolution and energy be developed, which being done, there is nothing which may not be accomplished. The weakest soul, knowing its own weakness, and believing this truth that strength can only be developed by effort and practise, will, thus believing, at once begin to exert itself, and, adding effort to effort, patience to patience, and strength to strength, will never cease to develop, and will at last grow divinely strong.

As the physically weak man can make himself strong by careful and patient training, so the man of weak thoughts can make them strong by exercising himself in right thinking.

To put away aimlessness and weakness, and to begin to think with purpose, is to enter the ranks of those strong ones who only recognize failure as one of the pathways to attainment; who make all conditions serve them, and who think strongly, attempt fearlessly, and accomplish masterfully.

Having conceived of his purpose, a man should mentally mark out a straight pathway to its achievement, looking neither to the right nor the left. Doubts and fears should be rigorously excluded; they are disintegrating elements, which break up the straight line of effort, rendering it crooked, ineffectual, useless. Thoughts of doubt and fear never accomplished anything, and never can. They always lead to failure. Purpose, energy, power to do, and all strong thoughts cease when doubt and fear creep in.

The will to do springs from the knowledge that we can do. Doubt and fear are the great enemies of knowledge, and he who encourages them, who does not slay them, thwarts himself at every step.

He who has conquered doubt and fear has conquered failure. His every thought is allied with power, and all difficulties are bravely met and wisely overcome. His purposes are seasonably planted, and they bloom and bring forth fruit, which does not fall prematurely to the ground.

Thought allied fearlessly to purpose becomes creative force: he who knows this is ready to become something higher and stronger than a mere bundle of wavering thoughts and fluctuating sensations; he who does this has become the conscious and intelligent wielder of his mental powers.

THE THOUGHT-FACTOR IN ACHIEVEMENT

All that a man achieves and all that he fails to achieve is the direct result of his own thoughts. In a justly ordered universe, where loss of equipoise would mean total destruction, individual responsibility must be absolute. A man's weakness and strength, purity and impurity, are his own, and not another man's; they are brought about by himself, and not by another; and they can only be altered by himself, never by another. His condition is also his own, and not another man's. His suffering and his happiness are evolved from within. As he thinks, so he is; as he continues to think, so he remains.

A strong man cannot help a weaker man unless that weaker man is willing to be helped, and even then the weak man must become strong of himself; he must, by his own efforts, develop the strength which he admires in another. None but himself can alter his condition.

It has been usual for men to think and to say, 'Many men are slaves because one is an oppressor; let us hate the oppressor.' Now, however, there is amongst an increasing few a tendency to reverse this judgment, and to say, 'One man is an oppressor because many are slaves; let us despise the slaves.'

The truth is that oppressor and slave are co-operators in ignorance, and, while seeming to afflict each other, are in reality afflicting themselves. A perfect Knowledge perceives the action of law in the weakness of the oppressed and the misapplied power of the oppressor; a perfect Love, seeing the suffering, which both states entail, condemns neither; a perfect Compassion embraces both oppressor and oppressed.

He who has conquered weakness, and has put away all

selfish thoughts, belongs neither to oppressor nor oppressed. He is free.

A man can only rise, conquer, and achieve by lifting up his thoughts. He can only remain weak, and abject, and miserable by refusing to lift up his thoughts.

Before a man can achieve anything, even in worldly things, he must lift his thoughts above slavish animal indulgence. He may not, in order to succeed, give up all animality and selfishness, by any means; but a portion of it must, at least, be sacrificed. A man whose first thought is bestial indulgence could neither think clearly nor plan methodically; he could not find and develop his latent resources, and would fail in any undertaking.

Not having commenced to manfully control his thoughts, he is not in a position to control affairs and to adopt serious responsibilities. He is not fit to act independently and stand alone. But he is limited only by the thoughts, which he chooses.

There can be no progress, no achievement without sacrifice, and a man's worldly success will be in the measure that he sacrifices his confused animal thoughts, and fixes his mind on the development of his plans, and the strengthening of his resolution and self-reliance. And the higher he lifts his thoughts, the more manly, upright, and righteous he becomes, the greater will be his success, the more blessed and enduring will be his achievements.

The universe does not favour the greedy, the dishonest, the vicious, although on the mere surface it may sometimes appear to do so; it helps the honest, the magnanimous, the virtuous. All the great Teachers of the ages have declared this in varying forms, and to prove and know it a man has but to persist in making himself more and more virtuous by lifting up his thoughts.

Intellectual achievements are the result of thought consecrated to the search for knowledge, or for the beautiful and true in life and nature. Such achievements may be sometimes connected with vanity and ambition, but they are not the outcome of those characteristics; they are the natural outgrowth of long and arduous effort, and of pure and unselfish thoughts. Spiritual achievements are the consummation of holy aspirations. He who lives constantly in the conception of noble and lofty thoughts, who dwells upon all that is pure and unselfish, will, as surely as the sun reaches its zenith and the moon its full, become wise and noble in character, and rise into a position of influence and blessedness.

Achievement, of whatever kind, is the crown of effort, the diadem of thought. By the aid of self-control, resolution, purity, righteousness, and well-directed thought a man ascends; by the aid of animality, indolence, impurity, corruption, and confusion of thought a man descends.

A man may rise to high success in the world, and even to lofty altitudes in the spiritual realm, and again descend into weakness and wretchedness by allowing arrogant, selfish, and corrupt thoughts to take possession of him.

Victories attained by right thought can only be maintained by watchfulness. Many give way when success is assured, and rapidly fall back into failure.

All achievements, whether in the business, intellectual, or spiritual world, are the result of definitely directed thought, are governed by the same law and are of the same method; the only difference lies in the object of attainment.

He who would accomplish little must sacrifice little; he who would achieve much must sacrifice much; he who would attain highly must sacrifice greatly.

SECTION II

HOW TO STAY SUCCESSFUL

.6.

His Holiness the Dalai Lama

Why Leaders Should Be Mindful, Selfless, and Compassionate

His Holiness the Dalai Lama, the spiritual leader of Tibet, is one of the world's most revered Buddhist monks and teachers. Here, he discusses the essential qualities of good leaders.

~

Over the past nearly sixty years, I have engaged with many leaders of governments, companies, and other organizations, and I have observed how our societies have developed and changed. I am happy to share some of my observations in case others may benefit from what I have learned.

Leaders, whatever field they work in, have a strong impact on people's lives and on how the world develops. We should remember that we are visitors on this planet. We are here for ninety or hundred years at the most. During this time, we should work to leave the world a better place.

What might a better world look like? I believe the answer is straightforward: a better world is one where people are happier. Why? Because all human beings want to be happy, and no one wants to suffer. Our desire for happiness is something we all have in common.

But today, the world seems to be facing an emotional crisis. Rates of stress, anxiety, and depression are higher than ever. The gap between rich and poor and between CEOs and employees is at a historic high. And the focus on turning a profit often overrules a commitment to people, the environment, or society.

I consider our tendency to see each other in terms of 'us' and 'them' as stemming from ignorance of our interdependence. As participants in the same global economy, we depend on each other, while changes in the climate and the global environment affect us all. What's more, as human beings, we are physically, mentally, and emotionally the same.

Look at bees. They have no constitution, police, or moral training, but they work together in order to survive. Though they may occasionally squabble, the colony survives on the basis of cooperation. Human beings, on the other hand, have constitutions, complex legal systems, and police forces; we have remarkable intelligence and a great capacity for love and affection. Yet, despite our many extraordinary qualities, we seem less able to cooperate.

In organizations, people work closely together every day. But despite working together, many feel lonely and stressed. Even though we are social animals, there is a lack of responsibility towards each other. We need to ask ourselves what's going wrong.

I believe that our strong focus on material development and accumulating wealth has led us to neglect our basic human need for kindness and care. Reinstating a commitment to the oneness of humanity and altruism toward our brothers and sisters is fundamental for societies and organizations and their individuals to thrive in the long run. Every one of us has a responsibility to make this happen.

What can leaders do?

Be mindful

Cultivate peace of mind. As human beings, we have a remarkable intelligence that allows us to analyze and plan for the future. We have language that enables us to communicate what we have understood to others. Since destructive emotions like anger and attachment cloud our ability to use our intelligence clearly, we need to tackle them.

Fear and anxiety easily give way to anger and violence. The opposite of fear is trust, which, related to warm-heartedness, boosts our self-confidence. Compassion also reduces fear, reflecting as it does a concern for others' well-being. This, not money and power, is what really attracts friends. When we're under the sway of anger or attachment, we're limited in our ability to take a full and realistic view of the situation. When the mind is compassionate, it is calm and we're able to use our sense of reason practically, realistically, and with determination.

Be selfless

We are naturally driven by self-interest; it's necessary to survive. But we need wise self-interest that is generous and cooperative, taking others' interests into account. Cooperation comes from friendship, friendship comes from trust, and trust comes from kind-heartedness. Once you have a genuine sense of concern for others, there's no room for cheating, bullying, or exploitation; instead, you can be honest, truthful, and transparent in your conduct.

Be compassionate

The ultimate source of a happy life is warm-heartedness. Even animals display some sense of compassion. When it comes to human beings, compassion can be combined with intelligence. Through the application of reason, compassion can be extended to all seven billion human beings. Destructive emotions are related to ignorance, while compassion is a constructive emotion related to intelligence. Consequently, it can be taught and learned.

The source of a happy life is within us. Troublemakers in many parts of the world are often quite well-educated, so it is not just education that we need. What we need is to pay attention to inner values.

The distinction between violence and non-violence lies less in the nature of a particular action and more in the motivation behind the action. Actions motivated by anger and greed tend to be violent, whereas those motivated by compassion and concern for others are generally peaceful. We won't bring about peace in the world merely by praying for it; we have to take steps to tackle the violence and corruption that disrupt peace. We can't expect change if we don't take action.

Peace also means being undisturbed, free from danger. It relates to our mental attitude and whether we have a calm mind. What is crucial to realize is that, ultimately, peace of mind is within us; it requires that we develop a warm heart and use our intelligence. People often don't realize that warm-heartedness, compassion, and love are actually factors for our survival.

Buddhist tradition describes three styles of compassionate leadership: the trailblazer, who leads from the front, takes risks, and sets an example; the ferryman, who accompanies those in his care and shapes the ups and downs of the crossing; and the shepherd, who sees every one of his flock into safety before himself. Three styles, three approaches, but what they have in common is an all-encompassing concern for the welfare of those they lead.

.7.

Dale Carnegie

How to Win Friends and Influence People

Dale Carnegie demonstrates why you should never tell a person they are wrong.

~

A SURE WAY OF MAKING ENEMIES—AND HOW TO AVOID IT

When Theodore Roosevelt was in the White House, he confessed that if he could be right seventy-five per cent of the time, he would reach the highest measure of his expectation.

If that was the highest rating that one of the most distinguished men of the twentieth century could hope to obtain, what about you and me?

If you can be sure of being right only fifty-five per cent of the time, you can go down to Wall Street and make a million dollars a day. If you can't be sure of being right even fifty-five per cent of the time, why should you tell other people they are wrong?

You can tell people they are wrong by a look or an intonation or a gesture just as eloquently as you can in words—and if you tell them they are wrong, do you make them want to agree with you? Never! For you have struck a direct blow at their intelligence, judgment, pride and self-respect. That will make them want to strike back. But it will never make them want to change their minds. You may then hurl at them all the logic of a Plato or an Immanuel Kant, but you will not alter their opinions, for you have hurt their feelings.

Never begin by announcing 'I am going to prove so-and-so to you.' That's bad. That's tantamount to saying: 'I'm smarter than you are, I'm going to tell you a thing or two and make you change your mind.'

That is a challenge. It arouses opposition and makes the listener want to battle with you before you even start.

It is difficult, under even the most benign conditions, to change people's minds. So why make it harder? Why handicap yourself?

If you are going to prove anything, don't let anybody know it. Do it so subtly, so adroitly, that no one will feel that you are doing it. This was expressed succinctly by Alexander Pope:

> Men must be taught as if you taught them not, and things unknown proposed as things forgot.

Over three hundred years ago Galileo said:

> You cannot teach a man anything; you can only help him to find it within himself.

As Lord Chesterfield said to his son:

> Be wiser than other people if you can; but do not tell them so.

Socrates said repeatedly to his followers in Athens:

> One thing only I know, and that is that I know nothing.

Well, I can't hope to be any smarter than Socrates, so I have quit telling people they are wrong. And I find that it pays.

If a person makes a statement that you think is wrong—yes, even that you know is wrong—isn't it better to begin by saying: 'Well, now, look, I thought otherwise, but I may be wrong. I frequently am. And if I am wrong, I want to be put right. Let's examine the facts.'

There's magic, positive magic, in such phrases as: 'I may be wrong. I frequently am. Let's examine the facts.'

Nobody in the heavens above or on earth beneath or in the waters under the earth will ever object to your saying: 'I may be wrong. Let's examine the facts.'

One of our class members who used this approach in dealing with customers was Harold Reinke, a Dodge dealer in Billings, Montana. He reported that because of the pressures of the automobile business, he was often hard-boiled and callous when dealing with customers' complaints. This caused flared tempers, loss of business and general unpleasantness.

He told his class: 'Recognizing that this was getting me nowhere fast, I tried a new tack. I would say something like this: "Our dealership has made so many mistakes that I am frequently ashamed. We may have erred in your case. Tell me about it."

'This approach becomes quite disarming, and by the

time the customer releases his feelings, he is usually much more reasonable when it comes to settling the matter. In fact, several customers have thanked me for having such an understanding attitude. And two of them have even brought in friends to buy new cars. In this highly competitive market, we need more of this type of customer, and I believe that showing respect for all customers' opinions and treating them diplomatically and courteously will help beat the competition.'

You will never get into trouble by admitting that you may be wrong. That will stop all argument and inspire your opponent to be just as fair and open and broad-minded as you are. It will make him want to admit that he, too, may be wrong.

If you know positively that a person is wrong, and you bluntly tell him or her so, what happens? Let me illustrate. Mr S—a young New York attorney, once argued a rather important case before the United States Supreme Court (*Lustgarten v. Fleet Corporation* 280 U.S. 320). The case involved a considerable sum of money and an important question of law. During the argument, one of the Supreme Court justices said to him: 'The statute of limitations in admiralty law is six years, is it not?'

Mr S—stopped, stared at the Justice for a moment, and then said bluntly: 'Your Honour, there is no statute of limitations in admiralty.'

'A hush fell on the court,' said Mr S— as he related his experience to one of the author's classes, 'and the temperature in the room seemed to drop to zero. I was right. Justice— was wrong. And I had told him so. But did that make him friendly? No. I still believe that I had the law on my side.

And I know that I spoke better than I ever spoke before. But I didn't persuade. I made the enormous blunder of telling a very learned and famous man that he was wrong.'

Few people are logical. Most of us are prejudiced and biased. Most of us are blighted with preconceived notions, with jealousy, suspicion, fear, envy and pride. And most citizens don't want to change their minds about their religion or their haircut or communism or their favorite movie star. So, if you are inclined to tell people they are wrong, please read the following paragraph every morning before breakfast. It is from James Harvey Robinson's enlightening book *The Mind in the Making*.

> We sometimes find ourselves changing our minds without any resistance or heavy emotion, but if we are told we are wrong, we resent the imputation and harden our hearts. We are incredibly heedless in the formation of our beliefs, but find ourselves filled with an illicit passion for them when anyone proposes to rob us of their companionship. It is obviously not the ideas themselves that are dear to us, but our self-esteem which is threatened.... The little word 'my' is the most important one in human affairs, and properly to reckon with it is the beginning of wisdom. It has the same force whether it is 'my' dinner, 'my' dog, and 'my' house, or 'my' father, 'my' country, and 'my' God. We not only resent the imputation that our watch is wrong, or our car shabby, but that our conception of the canals of Mars, of the pronunciation of 'Epictetus,' of the medicinal value of salicin, or of the date of Sargon I

> is subject to revision. We like to continue to believe what we have been accustomed to accept as true, and the resentment aroused when doubt is cast upon any of our assumptions leads us to seek every manner of excuse for clinging to it. The result is that most of our so-called reasoning consists in finding arguments for going on believing as we already do.

Carl Rogers, the eminent psychologist, wrote in his book *On Becoming a Person*:

> I have found it of enormous value when I can permit myself to understand the other person. The way in which I have worded this statement may seem strange to you. Is it necessary to permit oneself to understand another? I think it is. Our first reaction to most of the statements (which we hear from other people) is an evaluation or judgment, rather than an understanding of it. When someone expresses some feeling, attitude or belief, our tendency is almost immediately to feel 'that's right,' or 'that's stupid,' 'that's abnormal,' 'that's unreasonable,' 'that's incorrect,' 'that's not nice.' Very rarely do we permit ourselves to understand precisely what the meaning of the statement is to the other person.*

I once employed an interior decorator to make some draperies for my home. When the bill arrived, I was dismayed.

---

*Adapted from Carl R. Rogers, *On Becoming a Person*, Boston: Houghton Mifflin, 1961, p. 18ff.

A few days later, a friend dropped in and looked at the draperies. The price was mentioned, and she exclaimed with a note of triumph: 'What? That's awful. I am afraid he put one over on you.'

True? Yes, she had told the truth, but few people like to listen to truths that reflect on their judgment. So, being human, I tried to defend myself. I pointed out that the best is eventually the cheapest, that one can't expect to get quality and artistic taste at bargain-basement prices, and so on and on.

The next day another friend dropped in, admired the draperies, bubbled over with enthusiasm, and expressed a wish that she could afford such exquisite creations for her home. My reaction was totally different. 'Well, to tell the truth,' I said, 'I can't afford them myself. I paid too much. I'm sorry I ordered them.'

When we are wrong, we may admit it to ourselves. And if we are handled gently and tactfully, we may admit it to others and even take pride in our frankness and broad-mindedness. But not if someone else is trying to ram the unpalatable fact down our esophagus.

Horace Greeley, the most famous editor in America during the time of the Civil War, disagreed violently with Lincoln's policies. He believed that he could drive Lincoln into agreeing with him by a campaign of argument, ridicule and abuse. He waged this bitter campaign month after month, year after year. In fact, he wrote a brutal, bitter, sarcastic and personal attack on President Lincoln the night Booth shot him.

But did all this bitterness make Lincoln agree with

Greeley? Not at all. Ridicule and abuse never do.

If you want some excellent suggestions about dealing with people and managing yourself and improving your personality, read Benjamin Franklin's autobiography—one of the most fascinating life stories ever written, one of the classics of American literature. Ben Franklin tells how he conquered the iniquitous habit of argument and transformed himself into one of the most able, suave and diplomatic men in American history. One day, when Ben Franklin was a blundering youth, an old Quaker friend took him aside and lashed him with a few stinging truths, something like this:

> Ben, you are impossible. Your opinions have a slap in them for everyone who differs with you. They have become so offensive that nobody cares for them. Your friends find they enjoy themselves better when you are not around. You know so much that no man can tell you anything. Indeed, no man is going to try, for the effort would lead only to discomfort and hard work. So you are not likely ever to know any more than you do now, which is very little.

One of the finest things I know about Ben Franklin is the way he accepted that smarting rebuke. He was big enough and wise enough to realize that it was true, to sense that he was headed for failure and social disaster. So he made a right-about-face. He began immediately to change his insolent, opinionated ways.

'I made it a rule,' said Franklin, 'to forbear all direct contradiction to the sentiment of others, and all positive assertion of my own, I even forbade myself the use of every word or expression in the language that imported a fix'd opinion, such as "certainly," "undoubtedly," etc., and I adopted, instead of them, "I conceive," "I apprehend," or "I imagine" a thing to be so or so, or "it so appears to me at present." When another asserted something that I thought an error, I deny'd myself the pleasure of contradicting him abruptly, and of showing immediately some absurdity in his proposition: and in answering I began by observing that in certain cases or circumstances his opinion would be right, but in the present case there appear'd or seem'd to me some difference, etc. I soon found the advantage of this change in my manner; the conversations I engag'd in went on more pleasantly. The modest way in which I propos'd my opinions procur'd them a readier reception and less contradiction; I had less mortification when I was found to be in the wrong, and I more easily prevaile'd with others to give up their mistakes and join with me when I happened to be in the right.

'And this mode, which I at first put on with some violence to natural inclination, became at length so easy, and so habitual to me, that perhaps for these fifty years past no one has ever heard a dogmatical expression escape me. And to this habit (after my character of integrity) I think it principally owing that I had earned so much weight with my fellow citizens when I proposed new institutions, or alterations in the old, and so much influence in public councils when I became a member; for I was but a bad speaker, never eloquent, subject to much hesitation in my choice of words, hardly correct in language, and yet I generally carried my points.'

How do Ben Franklin's methods work in business? Let's take two examples.

Katherine A. Allred of Kings Mountain, North Carolina, is an industrial engineering supervisor for a yarn-processing plant. She told one of our classes how she handled a sensitive problem before and after taking our training:

'Part of my responsibility,' she reported, 'deals with setting up and maintaining incentive systems and standards for our operators so they can make more money by producing more yarn. The system we were using had worked fine when we had only two or three different types of yarn, but recently we had expanded our inventory and capabilities to enable us to run more than twelve different varieties. The present system was no longer adequate to pay the operators fairly for the work being performed and give them an incentive to increase production. I had worked up a new system which would enable us to pay the operator by the class of yam she was running at any one particular time. With my new system in hand, I entered the meeting determined to prove to the management that my system was the right approach. I told them in detail how they were wrong and showed where they were being unfair and how I had all the answers they needed. To say the least, I failed miserably! I had become so busy defending my position on the new system that I had left them no opening to graciously admit their problems on the old one. The issue was dead.

'After several sessions of this course, I realized all too well where I had made my mistakes. I called another meeting and this time I asked where they felt their problems were. We discussed each point, and I asked them their opinions on which was the best way to proceed. With a few low-keyed suggestions, at proper intervals, I let them develop my system themselves. At the end of the meeting when I actually presented my system, they enthusiastically accepted it.

'I am convinced now that nothing good is accomplished and a lot of damage can be done if you tell a person straight out that he or she is wrong. You only succeed in stripping that person of self-dignity and making yourself an unwelcome part of any discussion.'

Let's take another example—and remember these cases I am citing are typical of the experiences of thousands of other people. R. V. Crowley was a salesman for a lumber company in New York. Crowley admitted that he had been telling hard-boiled lumber inspectors for years that they were wrong. And he had won the arguments too. But it hadn't done any good. 'For these lumber inspectors,' said Mr Crowley, 'are like baseball umpires. Once they make a decision, they never change it.'

Mr Crowley saw that his firm was losing thousands of dollars through the arguments he won. So while taking my course, he resolved to change tactics and abandon arguments. With what results? Here is the story as he told it to the fellow members of his class:

'One morning the phone rang in my office. A hot and bothered person at the other end proceeded to inform me that a car of lumber we had shipped into his plant was entirely unsatisfactory. His firm had stopped unloading and requested that we make immediate arrangements to remove the stock from their yard. After about one-fourth of the car had been unloaded, their lumber inspector reported that the lumber was running fifty-five per cent below grade. Under the circumstances, they refused to accept it.

'I immediately started for his plant and on the way turned over in my mind the best way to handle the situation. Ordinarily, under such circumstances, I should have quoted grading rules and tried, as a result of my own experience and knowledge as a lumber inspector, to convince the other inspector that the lumber was actually up to grade, and that he was misinterpreting the rules in his inspection. However, I thought I would apply the principles learned in this training.

'When I arrived at the plant, I found the purchasing agent and the lumber inspector in a wicked humor, both set for an argument and a fight. We walked out to the car that was being unloaded, and I requested that they continue to unload so that I could see how things were going. I asked the inspector to go right ahead and lay out the rejects, as he had been doing, and to put the good pieces in another pile.

'After watching him for a while it began to dawn on me that his inspection actually was much too strict and that he was misinterpreting the rules. This particular lumber was white pine, and I knew the inspector was thoroughly schooled in hard woods but not a competent, experienced inspector on white pine. White pine happened to be my own strong suit, but did I offer any objection to the way he was grading the lumber? None whatever. I kept on watching and gradually began to ask questions as to why certain pieces were not satisfactory. I didn't for one instant insinuate that the inspector was wrong. I emphasized that my only reason for asking was in order that we could give his firm exactly what they wanted in future shipments. wanted in future shipments.

'By asking questions in a very friendly, cooperative spirit, and insisting continually that they were right in laying out boards not satisfactory to their purpose, I got him warmed up, and the strained relations between us began to thaw and melt away. An occasional carefully put remark on my part gave birth to the idea in his mind that possibly some of these rejected pieces were actually within the grade that they had bought, and that their requirements demanded a more expensive grade. I was very careful, however, not to let him think I was making an issue of this point.

'Gradually his whole attitude changed. He finally admitted to me that he was not experienced on white pine and began to ask me questions about each piece as it came out of the car, I would explain why such a piece came within the grade specified, but kept on insisting that we did not want him to take it if it was unsuitable for their purpose. He finally got to the point where he felt guilty every time he put a piece in the rejected pile. And at last he saw that the mistake was on their part for not having specified as good a grade as they needed.

'The ultimate outcome was that he went through the entire carload again after I left, accepted the whole lot, and we received a check in full.

'In that one instance alone, a little tact, and the determination to refrain from telling the other man he was wrong, saved my company a substantial amount of cash, and it would be hard to place a money value on the good will that was saved.'

Martin Luther King was asked how, as a pacifist, he could be an admirer of Air Force General Daniel 'Chappie' James, then the nation's highest-ranking black officer. Dr

King replied, 'I judge people by their own principles—not by my own.'

In a similar way, General Robert E. Lee once spoke to the president of the Confederacy, Jefferson Davis, in the most glowing terms about a certain officer under his command. Another officer in attendance was astonished. 'General,' he said, 'do you not know that the man of whom you speak so highly is one of your bitterest enemies who misses no opportunity to malign you?' 'Yes,' replied General Lee, 'but the president asked my opinion of him; he did not ask for his opinion of me.'

By the way, I am not revealing anything new in this chapter. Two thousand years ago, Jesus said: 'Agree with thine adversary quickly.'

And 2,200 years before Christ was born, King Akhtoi of Egypt gave his son some shrewd advice—advice that is sorely needed today. 'Be diplomatic,' counseled the King. 'It will help you gain your point.'

In other words, don't argue with your customer or your spouse or your adversary. Don't tell them they are wrong, don't get them stirred up. Use a little diplomacy.

.8.

George S. Clason

The Richest Man in Babylon

George Clason was a businessman and writer whose book The Richest Man in Babylon *has been continuously in print for nearly 100 years and has sold millions of copies since it was first published in 1926. It has often been referred to as one of the finest books available on personal finance, wealth management, and wealth creation. Here, he provides insights into attracting good luck.*

~

Meet the Goddess of Good Luck

'If a man be lucky, there is no foretelling the possible extent of his good fortune. Pitch him into the Euphrates and like as not he will swim out with a pearl in his hand.'

–Babylonian proverb

The desire to be lucky is universal. It was just as strong in the breasts of men four thousand years ago in ancient Babylon as it is in the hearts of men today. We all hope to be favoured by the whimsical Goddess of Good Luck. Is there some way we can meet her and attract, not only her favourable attention, but her generous favours?

Is there a way to attract good luck?

That is just what the men of ancient Babylon wished to know. It is exactly what they decided to find out. They were shrewd men and keen thinkers. That explains why their city became the richest and most powerful city of their time.

In that distant past, they had no schools or colleges. Nevertheless they had a centre of learning and a very practical one it was. Among the towered buildings in Babylon was one that ranked in importance with the Palace of the King, the Hanging Gardens and the temples of the Gods. You will find scant mention of it in the history books, more likely no mention at all, yet it exerted a powerful influence upon the thought of that time.

This building was the Temple of Learning where the wisdom of the past was expounded by voluntary teachers and where subjects of popular interest were discussed in open forums. Within its walls all men met as equals. The humblest of slaves could dispute with impunity the opinions of a prince of the royal house.

Among the many who frequented the Temple of Learning, was a wise rich man named Arkad, called the richest man in Babylon. He had his own special hall where almost any evening a large group of men, some old, some very young, but mostly middle-aged, gathered to discuss and argue interesting subjects. Suppose we listen in to see whether they knew how to attract good luck.

The sun had just set like a great red ball of fire shining

through the haze of desert dust when Arkad strolled to his accustomed platform. Already full four score men were awaiting his arrival, reclining on their small rugs spread upon the floor. More were still arriving.

'What shall we discuss this night?' Arkad inquired.

After a brief hesitation, a tall cloth weaver addressed him, arising as was the custom. 'I have a subject I would like to hear discussed yet hesitate to offer lest it seem ridiculous to you, Arkad, and my good friends here.'

Upon being urged to offer it, both by Arkad and by calls from the others, he continued: 'This day I have been lucky, for I have found a purse in which there are pieces of gold. To continue to be lucky is my great desire. Feeling that all men share with me this desire, I do suggest we debate how to attract good luck that we may discover ways it can be enticed to one.'

'A most interesting subject has been offered,' Arkad commented, 'one most worthy of our discussion. To some men, good luck bespeaks but a chance happening that, like an accident, may befall one without purpose or reason. Others do believe that the instigator of all good fortune is our most bounteous goddess, Ashtar, ever anxious to reward with generous gifts those who please her. Speak up, my friends, what say you, shall we seek to find if there be means by which good luck may be enticed to visit each and all of us?'

'Yea! Yea! And much of it!' responded the growing group of eager listeners.

Thereupon Arkad continued, 'To start our discussion, let us first hear from those among us who have enjoyed experiences similar to that of the cloth weaver in finding or receiving, without effort upon their part, valuable treasures or jewels.'

There was a pause in which all looked about expecting someone to reply but no one did.

'What, no one?' Arkad asked. 'Then rare indeed must be this kind of good luck. Who now will offer a suggestion as to where we shall continue our search?'

'That I will do,' spoke a well-robed young man, arising. 'When a man speaketh of luck is it not natural that his thoughts turn to the gaming tables? Is it not there we find many men courting the favour of the goddess in hope she will bless them with rich winnings?'

As he resumed his seat a voice called, 'Do not stop! Continue thy story! Tell us, didst thou find favour with the goddess at the gaming tables? Did she turn the cubes with red side up so thou filled thy purse at the dealer's expense or did she permit the blue sides to come up so the dealer raked in thy hard-earned pieces of silver?'

The young man joined the good-natured laughter, then replied, 'I am not averse to admitting she seemed not to know I was even there. But how about the rest of you? Have you found her waiting about such places to roll the cubes in your favour? We are eager to hear as well as to learn.'

'A wise start,' broke in Arkad. 'We meet here to consider all sides of each question. To ignore the gaming table would be to overlook an instinct common to most men, the love of taking a chance with a small amount of silver in the hope of winning much gold.'

'That doth remind me of the races but yesterday,' called out another listener. 'If the goddess frequents the gaming tables, certainly she dost not overlook the races where the gilded chariots and the foaming horses offer far more excitement. Tell us honestly, Arkad, didst she whisper to you to place your bet upon those gray horses from Nineveh yesterday? I was standing just behind thee and could scarce believe my ears when I heard thee place thy bet upon the grays. Thou knowest as well as any of us that no team in all Assyria can beat our beloved bays in a fair race.

'Didst the goddess whisper in thy ear to bet upon the grays because at the last turn the inside black would stumble and so interfere with our bays that the grays would win the race and score an unearned victory?'

Arkad smiled indulgently at the banter. 'What reason have we to feel the good goddess would take that much interest in any man's bet upon a horse race? To me she is a goddess of love and dignity whose pleasure it is to aid those who are in need and to reward those who are deserving. I look to find her, not at the gaming tables or the races where men lose more gold than they win but in other places where the doings of men are more worthwhile and more worthy of reward.

'In tilling the soil, in honest trading, in all of man's occupations, there is opportunity to make a profit upon his efforts and his transactions. Perhaps not all the time will he be rewarded because sometimes his judgment may be faulty, and other times the winds and the weather may defeat his efforts. Yet, if he persists, he may usually expect to realize his profit. This is so because the chances of profit are always in his favour.

'But, when a man playeth the games, the situation is

reversed for the chances of profit are always against him and always in favour of the game keeper. The game is so arranged that it will always favour the keeper. It is his business at which he plans to make a liberal profit for himself from the coins bet by the players. Few players realize how certain are the game keeper's profits and how uncertain are their own chances to win.

'For example, let us consider wagers placed upon the cube. Each time it is cast we bet which side will be uppermost. If it be the red side the game master pays to us four times our bet. But if any other of the five sides come uppermost, we lose our bet. Thus the figures show that for each cast we have five chances to lose, but because the red pays four for one, we have four chances to win. In a night's play the game master can expect to keep for his profit one-fifth of all the coins wagered. Can a man expect to win more than occasionally against odds so arranged that he should lose one-fifth of all his bets?'

'Yet some men do win large sums at times,' volunteered one of the listeners.

'Quite so, they do,' Arkad continued. 'Realizing this, the question comes to me whether money secured in such ways brings permanent value to those who are thus lucky. Among my acquaintances are many of the successful men of Babylon, yet among them I am unable to name a single one who started his success from such a source.

'You who are gathered here tonight know many more of our substantial citizens. To me it would be of much interest to learn how many of our successful citizens can credit the gaming tables with their start to success. Suppose each of you tell of those you know. What say you?'

After a prolonged silence, a wag ventured, 'Wouldst thy inquiry include the game keepers?'

'If you think of no one else,' Arkad responded. 'If not one of you can think of anyone else, then how about yourselves? Are there any consistent winners with us who hesitate to advise such a source for their incomes?'

His challenge was answered by a series of groans from the rear taken up and spread amid much laughter.

'It would seem we are not seeking good luck in such places as the goddess frequents,' he continued, 'Therefore let us explore other fields. We have not found it in picking up lost wallets. Neither have we found it haunting the gaming tables. As to the races, I must confess to have lost far more coins there than I have ever won.

'Now, suppose we consider our trades and businesses! Is it not natural if we conclude a profitable transaction to consider it not good luck but a just reward for our efforts? I am inclined to think we may be overlooking the gifts of the goddess. Perhaps she really does assist us when we do not appreciate her generosity. Who can suggest further discussion?'

Thereupon an elderly merchant arose, smoothing his genteel white robe. 'With thy permission, most honourable Arkad and my friends, I offer a suggestion. If, as you have said, we take credit to our own industry and ability for our business success, why not consider the successes we almost enjoyed but which escaped us, happenings which would have been most profitable. They would have been rare examples of good luck if they had actually happened. Because they were not brought to fulfilment we cannot consider them as our just rewards. Surely many men here have such experiences to relate.'

'Here is a wise approach,' Arkad approved. 'Who among you have had good luck within your grasp only to see it escape?'

Many hands were raised, among them that of the merchant. Arkad motioned to him to speak. 'As you suggested this approach, we should like to hear first from you.'

'I will gladly relate a tale,' he resumed, 'that doth illustrate how closely, unto a man good luck may approach and how blindly he may permit it to escape, much to his loss and later regret.

'Many years ago, when I was a young man, just married and well-started to earning, my father did come one day and urge most strongly that I enter upon an investment. The son of one of his good friends had taken notice of a barren tract of land not far beyond the outer walls of our city. It lay high above the canal where no water could reach it.

'The son of my father's friend devised a plan to purchase this land, build three large waterwheels that could be operated by oxen and thereby raise the life-giving waters to the fertile soil. This accomplished, he planned to divide it into small tracts and sell to the residents of the city for herb patches.

'The son of my father's friend did not possess sufficient gold to complete such an undertaking. Like myself, he was a young man earning a fair sum. His father, like mine, was a man of large family and small means. He, therefore, decided to interest a group of men to enter the enterprise with him. The group was to comprise twelve, each of whom must be a money earner and agree to pay one-tenth of his earnings into the enterprise until the land was made ready for sale. All would then share justly in the profits in proportion to their investment.

'"Thou, my son," bespoke my father unto me, "art now in thy young manhood. It is my deep desire that thou begin the building of a valuable estate for thyself that thou mayest become respected among men. I desire to see thou profit from a knowledge of the thoughtless mistakes of thy father."

'"This do I most ardently desire, my father," I replied.

'"Then, this do I advise. Do what I should have done at thy age. From thy earnings keep out one-tenth to put into favourable investments. With this one-tenth of thy earnings and what it will also earn, thou canst, before thou art my age, accumulate for thyself a valuable estate."

'"Thy words are words of wisdom, my father. Greatly do I desire riches. Yet there are many uses to which my earnings are called. Therefore, do I hesitate to do as thou dost advise. I am young. There is plenty of time."

'"So I thought at thy age, yet behold, many years have passed and I have not yet made the beginning."

'"We live in a different age, my father. I shall avoid thy mistakes."

'"Opportunity stands before thee, my son. It is offering a chance that may lead to wealth. I beg of thee, do not delay. Go upon the morrow to the son of my friend and bargain with him to pay ten percent of thy earnings into this investment. Go promptly upon the morrow. Opportunity waits for no man. Today it is here; soon it is gone. Therefore, delay not!"

'In spite of the advice of my father, I did hesitate. There

were beautiful new robes just brought by the tradesmen from the East, robes of such richness and beauty my good wife and I felt we must each possess one. Should I agree to pay one-tenth of my earnings into the enterprise, we must deprive ourselves of these and other pleasures we dearly desired. I delayed making a decision until it was too late, much to my subsequent regret. The enterprise did prove to be more profitable than any man had prophesied. This is my tale, showing how I did permit good luck to escape.'

'In this tale we see how good luck waits to come to that man who accepts opportunity,' commented a swarthy man of the desert. 'To the building of an estate there must always be the beginning. That start may be a few pieces of gold or silver which a man diverts from his earnings to his first investment. I, myself, am the owner of many herds. The start of my herds I did begin when I was a mere boy and did purchase with one piece of silver a young calf. This, being the beginning of my wealth, was of great importance to me.

'To take his first start to building an estate is as good luck as can come to any man. With all men, that first step, which changes them from men who earn from their own labour to men who draw dividends from the earnings of their gold, is important. Some, fortunately, take it when young and thereby outstrip in financial success those who do take it later or those unfortunate men, like the father of this merchant, who never take it.

'Had our friend, the merchant, taken this step in his early manhood when this opportunity came to him, this day he would be blessed with much more of this world's goods. Should the good luck of our friend, the cloth weaver, cause him to take such a step at this time, it will indeed be but the beginning of much greater good fortune.'

'Thank you! I like to speak, also.' A stranger from another country arose. 'I am a Syrian. Not so well do I speak your tongue. I wish to call this friend, the merchant, a name. Maybe you think it not polite, this name. Yet I wish to call him that. But, alas, I not know your word for it. If I do call it in Syrian, you will not understand. Therefore, please some good gentlemen, tell me that right name you call man who puts off doing those things that mighty good for him.'

'Procrastinator,' called a voice.

'That's him,' shouted the Syrian, waving his hands excitedly, 'he accepts not opportunity when she comes. He waits. He says I have much business right now. Bye and bye I talk to you. Opportunity, she will not wait for such slow fellow. She thinks if a man desires to be lucky he will step quick. Any man who not step quick when opportunity comes, he big procrastinator like our friend, this merchant.'

The merchant arose and bowed good-naturedly in response to the laughter. 'My admiration to thee, stranger within our gates, who hesitates not to speak the truth.'

'And now let us hear another tale of opportunity. Who has for us another experience?' demanded Arkad.

'I have,' responded a red-robed man of middle age. 'I am a buyer of animals, mostly camels and horses. Sometimes I do also buy the sheep and goats. The tale I am about to relate will tell truthfully how opportunity came one night when I did least expect it. Perhaps for this reason I did let it escape. Of this you shall be the judge.

'Returning to the city one evening after a disheartening

ten-days' journey in search of camels, I was much angered to find the gates of the city closed and locked. While my slaves spread our tent for the night, which we looked to spend with little food and no water, I was approached by an elderly farmer who, like ourselves, found himself locked outside.

'"Honoured sir," he addressed me, "from thy appearance, I do judge thee to be a buyer. If this be so, much would I like to sell to thee the most excellent flock of sheep just driven up. Alas, my good wife lies very sick with the fever. I must return with all haste. Buy thou my sheep that I and my slaves may mount our camels and travel back without delay."

'So dark it was that I could not see his flock, but from the bleating I did know it must be large. Having wasted ten days searching for camels I could not find, I was glad to bargain with him. In his anxiety, he did set a most reasonable price. I accepted, well knowing my slaves could drive the flock through the city gates in the morning and sell at a substantial profit.

'The bargain concluded, I called my slaves to bring torches that we might count the flock which the farmer declared to contain nine hundred. I shall not burden you, my friends, with a description of our difficulty in attempting to count so many thirsty, restless, milling sheep. It proved to be an impossible task. Therefore, I bluntly informed the farmer I would count them at daylight and pay him then.

'"Please, most honourable sir" he pleaded, "pay me but two-thirds of the price tonight that I may be on my way. I will leave my most intelligent and educated slave to assist to make the count in the morning. He is trustworthy and to him thou canst pay the balance."

'But I was stubborn and refused to make payment that night. Next morning, before I awoke, the city gates opened and four buyers rushed out in search of flocks. They were most eager and willing to pay high prices because the city was threatened with siege, and food was not plentiful. Nearly three times the price at which he had offered the flock to me did the old farmer receive for it. Thus was rare good luck allowed to escape.'

'Here is a tale most unusual,' commented Arkad.

'What wisdom doth it suggest?'

'The wisdom of making a payment immediately when we are convinced our bargain is wise' suggested a venerable saddle-maker. 'If the bargain be good, then dost thou need protection against thy own weaknesses as much as against any other man. We mortals are changeable. Alas, I must say more apt to change our minds when right than wrong. Wrong, we are stubborn indeed. Right, we are prone to vacillate and let opportunity escape. My first judgment is my best. Yet always have I found it difficult to compel myself to proceed with a good bargain when made. Therefore, as a protection against my own weaknesses, I do make a prompt deposit thereon. This doth save me from later regrets for the good luck that should have been mine.'

'Thank you! Again I like to speak.' The Syrian was upon his feet once more. 'These tales much alike. Each time opportunity fly away for same reason. Each time she come to procrastinator, bringing good plan. Each time they hesitate, not say, right now best time, I do it quick. How can men succeed that way?'

'Wise are thy words, my friend,' responded the buyer. 'Good luck fled from procrastination in both these tales. Yet, this is not unusual. The spirit of procrastination is within all men. We desire riches; yet, how often when opportunity doth appear before us, that spirit of procrastination from within doth urge various delays in our acceptance. In listening to it we do become our own worst enemies.

'In my younger days I did not know it by this long word our friend from Syria doth enjoy. I did think at first it was my own poor judgment that did cause me loss of many profitable trades. Later, I did credit it to my stubborn disposition. At last, I did recognize it for what it was—a habit of needless delaying where action was required, action prompt and decisive. How I did hate it when its true character stood revealed. With the bitterness of a wild ass hitched to a chariot, I did break loose from this enemy to my success.'

'Thank you! I like ask question from Mr Merchant.' The Syrian was speaking. 'You wear fine robes, not like those of poor man. You speak like successful man. Tell us, do you listen now when procrastination whispers in your ear?'

'Like our friend the buyer, I also had to recognize and conquer procrastination,' responded the merchant. 'To me, it proved to be an enemy, ever watching and waiting to thwart my accomplishments. The tale I did relate is but one of many similar instances I could tell to show how it drove away my opportunities. 'Tis not difficult to conquer, once understood. No man willingly permits the thief to rob his bins of grain. Nor does any man willingly permit an enemy to drive away his customers and rob him of his profits. When once I did recognize that such acts as these my enemy was committing, with determination I conquered him. So must every man master his own spirit of procrastination before he can expect to share in the rich treasures of Babylon.

'What sayest, Arkad? Because thou art the richest man in Babylon, many do proclaim thee to be the luckiest. Dost agree with me that no man can arrive at a full measure of success until he hath completely crushed the spirit of procrastination within him?'

'It is even as thou sayest,' Arkad admitted. 'During my long life I have watched generation following generation, marching forward along those avenues of trade, science and learning that lead to success in life. Opportunities came to all these men. Some grasped theirs and moved steadily to the gratification of their deepest desires, but the majority hesitated, faltered and fell behind.'

Arkad turned to the cloth weaver. 'Thou didst suggest that we debate good luck. Let us hear what thou now thinkest upon the subject.'

'I do see good luck in a different light. I had thought of it as something most desirable that might happen to a man without effort upon his part. Now, I do realize such happenings are not the sort of thing one may attract to himself. From our discussion have I learned that to attract good luck to oneself, it is necessary to take advantage of opportunities. Therefore, in the future, I shall endeavour to make the best of such opportunities as do come to me.'

'Thou hast well grasped the truths brought forth in our discussion,' Arkad replied. 'Good luck, we do find, often follows opportunity but seldom comes otherwise. Our merchant friend would have found great good luck had he accepted the opportunity the good goddess did present to him. Our friend the buyer, likewise, would have enjoyed good luck had he completed the purchase of the flock and sold at such a handsome profit.

'We did pursue this discussion to find a means by which good luck could be enticed to us. I feel that we have found the way. Both the tales did illustrate how good luck follows opportunity. Herein lies a truth that many similar tales of good luck, won or lost, could not change. The truth is this: *Good luck can be enticed by accepting opportunity*.

'Those eager to grasp opportunities for their betterment, do attract the interest of the good goddess. She is ever anxious to aid those who please her. Men of action please her best.

'Action will lead thee forward to the successes thou dost desire.'

MEN OF ACTION ARE FAVOURED BY THE GODDESS OF GOOD LUCK

.9.

Napoleon Hill

Think and Grow Rich

This extract from Napoleon Hill's bestselling book Think and Grow Rich *emphasizes the importance of persistence.*

~

Persistence is a state of mind, therefore it can be cultivated. Like all states of mind, persistence is based upon definite causes, among them these:

a. DEFINITENESS OF PURPOSE. Knowing what one wants is the first and, perhaps, the most important step toward the development of persistence. A strong motive forces one to surmount many difficulties.
b. DESIRE. It is comparatively easy to acquire and to maintain persistence in pursuing the object of intense desire.
c. SELF-RELIANCE. Belief in one's ability to carry out a plan encourages one to follow the plan through with persistence....
d. DEFINITENESS OF PLANS. Organized plans, even though they may be weak and entirely impractical, encourage persistence.

e. ACCURATE KNOWLEDGE. Knowing that one's plans are sound, based upon experience or observation, encourages persistence; 'guessing' instead of 'knowing' destroys persistence.
f. CO-OPERATION. Sympathy, understanding, and harmonious cooperation with others tend to develop persistence.
g. WILL-POWER. The habit of concentrating one's thoughts upon the building of plans for the attainment of a definite purpose, leads to persistence.
h. HABIT. Persistence is the direct result of habit. The mind absorbs and becomes a part of the daily experiences upon which it feeds. Fear, the worst of all enemies, can be effectively cured by forced repetition of acts of courage. Everyone who has seen active service in war knows this.

Before leaving the subject of PERSISTENCE, take inventory of yourself and determine in what particular, if any, you are lacking in this essential quality. Measure yourself courageously, point by point, and see how many of the eight factors of persistence you lack. The analysis may lead to discoveries that will give you a new grip on yourself.

SYMPTOMS OF LACK OF PERSISTENCE

Here you will find the real enemies which stand between you and noteworthy achievement. Here you will find not only the 'symptoms' indicating weakness of PERSISTENCE, but also the deeply seated subconscious causes of this weakness. Study the list carefully, and face yourself squarely IF YOU REALLY

WISH TO KNOW WHO YOU ARE, AND WHAT YOU ARE CAPABLE OF DOING. These are the weaknesses which must be mastered by all who accumulate riches.

1. Failure to recognize and to clearly define exactly what one wants.
2. Procrastination, with or without cause. (Usually backed up with a formidable array of alibis and excuses).
3. Lack of interest in acquiring specialized knowledge.
4. Indecision, the habit of 'passing the buck' on all occasions, instead of facing issues squarely. (Also backed by alibis).
5. The habit of relying upon alibis instead of creating definite plans for the solution of problems.
6. Self-satisfaction. There is but little remedy for this affliction, and no hope for those who suffer from it.
7. Indifference, usually reflected in one's readiness to compromise on all occasions, rather than meet opposition and fight it.
8. The habit of blaming others for one's mistakes, and accepting unfavorable circumstances as being unavoidable.
9. WEAKNESS OF DESIRE, due to neglect in the choice of MOTIVES that impel action.
10. Willingness, even eagerness, to quit at the first sign of defeat....
11. Lack of ORGANIZED PLANS, placed in writing where they may be analyzed.
12. The habit of neglecting to move on ideas, or to grasp opportunity when it presents itself
13. WISHING instead of WILLING.
14. The habit of compromising with POVERTY instead of

aiming at riches. General absence of ambition to *be*, to *do*, and to *own*.

15. Searching for all the shortcuts to riches, trying to GET without GIVING a fair equivalent, usually reflected in the habit of gambling, endeavoring to drive 'sharp' bargains.
16. FEAR OF CRITICISM, failure to create plans and to put them into action, because of what other people will think, do, or say. This enemy belongs at the head of the list, because it generally exists in one's subconscious mind, where its presence is not recognized....

Let us examine some of the symptoms of the Fear of Criticism. The majority of people permit relatives, friends, and the public at large to so influence them that they cannot live their own lives because they fear criticism.

Huge numbers of people make mistakes in marriage, stand by the bargain, and go through life miserable and unhappy, because they fear criticism which may follow if they correct the mistake. (Anyone who has submitted to this form of fear knows the irreparable damage it does, by destroying ambition, self-reliance, and the desire to achieve).

Millions of people neglect to acquire belated educations, after having left school, because they fear criticism.

Countless numbers of men and women, both young and old, permit relatives to wreck their lives in the name of DUTY, because they fear criticism. (Duty does not require any person to submit to the destruction of his personal ambitions and the right to live his own life in his own way).

People refuse to take chances in business, because they fear the criticism which may follow if they fail. The fear of criticism, in such cases is stronger than the DESIRE for success.

Too many people refuse to set high goals for themselves, or even neglect selecting a career, because they fear the criticism of relatives and 'friends' who may say 'Don't aim so high, people will think you are crazy.'

When Andrew Carnegie suggested that I devote twenty years to the organization of a philosophy of individual achievement my first impulse of thought was fear of what people might say. The suggestion set up a goal for me far out of proportion to any I had ever conceived. As quick as a flash, my mind began to create alibis and excuses, all of them traceable to the inherent FEAR OF CRITICISM. Something inside of me said. 'You can't do it—the job is too big and requires too much time—what will your relatives think of you?—how will you earn a living?—no one has ever organized a philosophy of success, what right have you to believe you can do it? who are you, anyway, to aim so high?—remember your humble birth—what do you know about philosophy people will think you are crazy—(and they did)—why hasn't some other person done this before now?'

These, and many other questions flashed into my mind, and demanded attention. It seemed as if the whole world had suddenly turned its attention to me with the purpose of ridiculing me into giving up all desire to carry out Mr Carnegie's suggestion.

I had a fine opportunity, then and there, to kill off ambition before it gained control of me. Later in life, after having analyzed thousands of people, I discovered that MOST IDEAS ARE STILL-BORN, AND NEED THE

BREATH OF LIFE INJECTED INTO THEM THROUGH DEFINITE PLANS OF IMMEDIATE ACTION. The time to nurse an idea is at the time of its birth. Every minute it lives, gives it a better chance of surviving. The FEAR OF CRITICISM is at the bottom of the destruction of most ideas which never reach the PLANNING and ACTION stage.

Many people believe that material success is the result of favorable 'breaks.' There is an element of ground for the belief, but those depending entirely upon luck, are nearly always disappointed, because they overlook another important factor which must be present before one can be sure of success. It is the knowledge with which favorable 'breaks' can be made to order.

During the depression, W. C. Fields, the comedian, lost all his money, and found himself without income, without a job, and his means of earning a living (vaudeville) no longer existed. Moreover, he was past sixty, when many men consider themselves 'old.' He was so eager to stage a comeback that he offered to work without pay, in a new field (movies). In addition to his other troubles, he fell and injured his neck. To many that would have been the place to give up and QUIT. But Fields was PERSISTENT. He knew that if he carried on he would get the 'breaks' sooner or later, and he did get them, but not by chance.

Marie Dressler found herself down and out, with her money gone, with no job, when she was about sixty. She, too, went after the 'breaks,' and got them. Her PERSISTENCE brought an astounding triumph late in life, long beyond the age when most men and women are done with ambition to achieve.

Eddie Cantor lost his money in the 1929 stock crash, but he still had his PERSISTENCE and his courage. With these, plus two prominent eyes, he exploited himself back into an income of $10,000 a week! Verily, if one has PERSISTENCE, one can get along very well without many other qualities.

The only 'break' anyone can afford to rely upon is a self-made 'break.' These come through the application of PERSISTENCE. The starting point is DEFINITENESS OF PURPOSE.

Examine the first hundred people you meet, ask them what they want most in life, and ninety-eight of them will not be able to tell you. If you press them for an answer, some will say - SECURITY, many will say - MONEY, a few will say - HAPPINESS, others will say - FAME AND POWER, and still others will say - SOCIAL RECOGNITION, EASE IN LIVING, ABILITY TO SING, DANCE, or WRITE, but none of them will be able to define these terms, or give the slightest indication of a PLAN by which they hope to attain these vaguely expressed wishes. Riches do not respond to wishes. They respond only to definite plans, backed by definite desires, through constant PERSISTENCE.

HOW TO DEVELOP PERSISTENCE

There are four simple steps which lead to the habit of PERSISTENCE. They call for no great amount of intelligence, no particular amount of education, and but little time or effort. The necessary steps are:

1. A DEFINITE PURPOSE BACKED BY BURNING DESIRE FOR ITS FULFILLMENT.
2. A DEFINITE PLAN, EXPRESSED IN CONTINUOUS ACTION.
3. A MIND CLOSED TIGHTLY AGAINST ALL NEGATIVE AND DISCOURAGING INFLUENCES, including negative suggestions of relatives, friends and acquaintances.
4. A FRIENDLY ALLIANCE WITH ONE OR MORE PERSONS WHO WILL ENCOURAGE ONE TO FOLLOW THROUGH WITH BOTH PLAN AND PURPOSE.

These four steps are essential for success in all walks of life. The entire purpose of the thirteen principles of this philosophy is to enable one to take these four steps as a matter of habit.

These are the steps by which one may control one's economic destiny. They are the steps that lead to freedom and independence of thought. They are the steps that lead to riches, in small or great quantities. They lead the way to power, fame, and worldly recognition. They are the four steps which guarantee favorable 'breaks.' They are the steps that convert dreams into physical realities. They lead, also, to the mastery of FEAR, DISCOURAGEMENT, INDIFFERENCE.

There is a magnificent reward for all who learn to take these four steps. It is the privilege of writing one's own ticket, and of making Life yield whatever price is asked.

.10.

Devdutt Pattanaik

The Success Sutra

In this extract, Devdutt Pattanaik describes the path to sustainable wealth.

~

Regeneration ensures sustainable wealth

Vishnu's most popular avatar is Krishna and Krishna's abode is called Goloka, the pastureland, which is full of cows that gather around Krishna who enthralls them with the music of his flute. These cows are not tethered and do not need to be. They give their milk to Krishna joyously, continuously and voluntarily.

Cows feed on grass which when eaten grows back, making grass a renewable raw material. The story goes that a pot containing amrit was placed on the grass a long time ago, enabling it to regenerate itself. With an assured and sustainable source of food, the cow is able to give a sustained supply of milk. This makes the cow and grass symbols of sustainable and regenerating resources, which makes them sacred and an integral part of Hindu and Jain rituals.

It is very easy to see this story literally: as an appeal for a vegetarian lifestyle, or as an endorsement for protecting cows. But the message is more symbolic: it reaffirms the need to secure a sustainable livelihood. This is why the gift of the cow, go-daan, is the greatest of gifts. It makes a man autonomous; he depends on no one for food (milk) or fuel (dung).

People are advised to give so many cows that the depression left behind as a result of the dust kicked up by the gifted cows turns into a lake which sustains more life. Go-daan is an appeal to create more means of livelihood that sustain more households. Go-hatya, or killing a cow thereby destroying a man's livelihood, is the greatest of crimes.

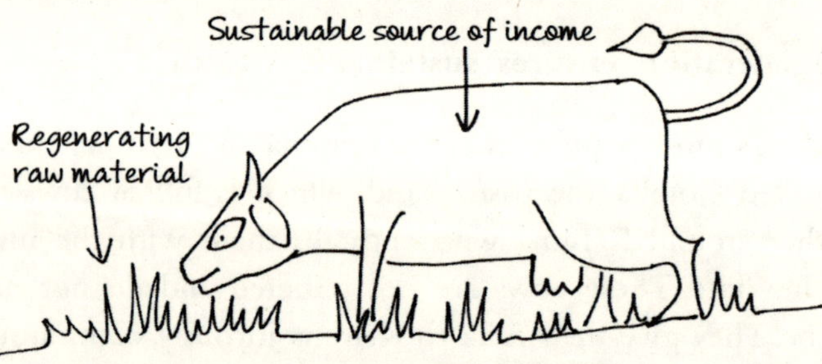

In Vishnu temples, Vishnu's mount, the eagle Garud, is shown holding a naga, or serpent, in his talons. It is an acknowledgement of the violence inherent in feeding. But the devotee is repeatedly told that the naga is immortal. The nagas slithered over the grass on which the amrit was kept and so they, too, possess the power to regenerate themselves like grass.

Vishnu is, thus, associated with the cow and the eagle, both of which consume what is in the mythological world considered renewable food sources. Regeneration is the key to sustainability. Words like regeneration and renewal are thus intrinsic to the yagna. They compensate for the harm done by violence.

Paresh-bhai noticed his son, Raghu, negotiating a price with the tempo owner. He saw the sense of triumph Raghu felt when he managed to bring down the price by another 10 per cent. Paresh-bhai, instead of congratulating Raghu, warned him, 'If he runs out of business, we will lose a very good and honest transporter for our goods. In trying to improve your margin, you are destroying his very livelihood. He is already in debt. We need our vendors to survive and thrive so that they can support our business. If we grow at the cost of our vendors, we will do well for a short time, but then collapse. They will either shut down their business or rush to aid the competition as soon as it arrives.' Paresh-bhai knows the value of regenerating serpents and regenerating grass.

Restraint ensures regeneration

After harvest, for the land to restore its fertility, the farmer has to leave the land fallow. During spawning season, the fisherman must not go fishing so that he has enough fish to catch the rest of the year. Restraint is the key to regeneration and hence, also, sustainability.

Shiva is the god of restraint. He knows the secret of outgrowing hunger. Unlike Indra who only wants amrit,

Shiva has the power to consume halahal, or the poison that accompanies amrit when the devas churn the ocean of milk. This is a metaphor for industrial waste that is a natural outcome of industrial activities. Indra does not care about the waste. But Shiva pays full attention to it; finding ways of containing, and even consuming it, so that the poison does not end up destroying the world. Without Shiva, the devas would not have access to amrit.

The devas, however, do not know the value Shiva brings to their lives, they remain wary of tapasvis. They prefer entertainment to introspection any day.

While the devas kill asuras, the asuras have the power to be reborn, thanks to Shiva. He gives them sanjivani vidya, the power to come back to life. The farmer may clear the forest, but sooner than later the weeds and floods come back. These weeds and floods play a key role in the regeneration of soil. Like the farmer who resents the weeds and floods, Indra resents the asuras who keep attacking Amravati at periodic intervals. He does not like Shiva helping them with sanjivani vidya. He imagines a world where every plant is a crop, existing solely for the satisfaction of his own hunger.

The asuras do tapasya to become more powerful, not wiser.

They worship Shiva as a source of power, and pay scant regard to his wisdom.

Only Vishnu knows the value of Shiva. He realizes that while performing a yagna externally to generate Narayani, the yajaman has to simultaneously perform tapasya internally and invoke Narayan if he wishes to have regenerating resources and a sustainable business.

That is why the Veda keeps referring to the yagna-purush that has to be sacrificed during the yagna. While agni, the fire in the altar, burns resources externally, tapa, the fire in the mind, needs to burn the yajaman's ignorance. This needs to occur simultaneously with the ritual. Only then can there be intellectual growth along with emotional and material growth. If the yagna does not provoke intellectual and emotional growth in the yajaman, material growth will be indiscriminate and that will herald the floods of Pralay.

Pranita was always careful about money. She wanted to ensure that her children got a good education and lived a comfortable life. When she was forty, her fortunes changed. Her business started to boom. She began earning much more than her husband. 'Now you can buy the jewellery that you never bought,' her husband said jokingly. Pranita smiled. She never bought jewellery not because she could not afford it but because she never desired it. Why should the availability of money change that about her? Why should extra resources make her change her comfortable lifestyle? Money for her was simply a tool of comfort. She did not value people, including herself, for the money they had. This mindset allowed Pranita to use her money to invest in more businesses, both high-risk and low-return ones. Before she knew it, she had become a small investment banker partnering with an NGO, giving out micro-loans, helping women in the slums near her house, all the while maintaining a comfortable lifestyle and ensuring her children were well educated and happy. Pranita's tapasya had enabled her not to be swayed by wealth, which enabled her to perform a better yagna than others.

.11.

Joseph Murphy

The Power of Your Subconscious Mind

Joseph Murphy was an Irish author who spent a significant amount of time in India studying Hindu philosophy. His most famous book, The Power of Your Subconscious Mind, *has been a perennial bestseller in India and elsewhere. Here, he reveals the power of the subconscious in removing obstacles.*

~

HOW YOUR SUBCONSCIOUS REMOVES MENTAL BLOCKS

The solution lies within the problem. The answer is in every question. If you are presented with a difficult situation and you cannot see your way clear, the best procedure is to assume that infinite intelligence within your subconscious mind knows all and sees all, has the answer, and is revealing it to you now. Your new mental attitude that the creative intelligence is bringing about a happy solution will enable you to find the answer. Rest assured that such an attitude of mind would bring order, peace, and meaning to all your undertakings.

HOW TO BREAK OR BUILD A HABIT

You are a creature of habit. Habit is the function of your subconscious mind. You learned to swim, ride a bicycle, dance, and drive a car by consciously doing these things over and over again until they established tracks in your subconscious mind. Then, the automatic habit action of your subconscious mind took over. This is sometimes called second nature, which is a reaction of your subconscious mind to your thinking and acting. You are free to choose a good habit or a bad habit. If you repeat a negative thought or act over a period of time, you will be under the compulsion of a habit. The law of your subconscious is compulsion.

HOW HE BROKE A BAD HABIT

Mr Jones said to me, 'An uncontrollable urge to drink seizes me, and I remain drunk for two weeks at a time. I can't give up this terrible habit.'

Time and time again these experiences had occurred to this unfortunate man. He had grown into the habit of drinking to excess. Although he had started drinking of his own initiative, he also began to realize that he could change the habit and establish a new one. He said that while through his willpower he was able to suppress his desires temporarily, his continued efforts to suppress the many urges only made matters worse. His repeated failures convinced him that he was hopeless and powerless to control his urge or obsession. This idea of being powerless operated as a powerful suggestion to his subconscious mind and aggravated his weakness, making his life a succession of failures.

I taught him to harmonize the functions of the conscious and subconscious mind. When these two cooperate, the idea or desire implanted in the subconscious mind is realized. His reasoning mind agreed that if the old habit path or track had carried him into trouble, he could consciously form a new path to freedom, sobriety, and peace of mind. He knew that his destructive habit was automatic, but since it was acquired through his conscious choice, he realized that if he had been conditioned negatively, he also could be conditioned positively. As a result, he ceased thinking of the fact that he was powerless to overcome the habit. Moreover, he understood clearly that there was no obstacle to his healing other than his own thought. Therefore, there was no occasion for great mental effort or mental coercion.

THE POWER OF HIS MENTAL PICTURE

This man acquired a practice of relaxing his body and getting into a relaxed, drowsy, meditative state. Then he filled his mind with the picture of the desired end, knowing his subconscious mind could bring it about the easiest way. He imagined his daughter congratulating him on his freedom, and saying to him, 'Daddy, it's wonderful to have you home!' He had lost his family through drink. He was not allowed to visit them, and his wife would not speak to him. Regularly, systematically, he used to sit down and meditate in the way outlined. When his attention wandered, he made it a habit to immediately recall the mental picture of his daughter with her smile and the scene of his home enlivened by her cheerful voice. All this brought about a reconditioning of his mind. It was a gradual process. He kept it up. He persevered knowing that sooner or later he would establish a new habit pattern in his subconscious mind. I told him that he could liken his conscious mind to a camera, that his subconscious mind was the sensitive plate on which he registered and impressed the picture. This made a profound impression on him, and his whole aim was to firmly impress the picture on his mind and develop it there. Films are developed in the dark; likewise, mental pictures are developed in the darkroom of the subconscious mind.

FOCUSED ATTENTION

Realizing that his conscious mind was simply a camera, he used no effort. There was no mental struggle. He quietly adjusted his thoughts and focused his attention on the scene before him until he gradually became identified with the picture. He became absorbed in the mental atmosphere, repeating the mental movie frequently. There was no room for doubt that a healing would follow. When there was any temptation to drink, he would switch his imagination from any reveries of drinking bouts to the feeling of being at home with his family. He was successful because he confidently expected to experience the picture he was developing in his mind. Today he is president of a multi-million-dollar concern and is radiantly happy.

HE SAID A JINX WAS FOLLOWING HIM

Mr Block said that he had been making an annual income of $20,000, but for the past three months all doors seemed to jam tightly. He brought clients up to the point where they were about to sign on the dotted line, and then at the eleventh hour the door closed. He added that perhaps a jinx was following him. In discussing the matter with Mr Block, I discovered that three months previously he had become very irritated, annoyed, and resentful toward a dentist who, after he had promised to sign a contract, had withdrawn at the last moment. He began to live in the unconscious fear that other clients would do the same, thereby setting up a history of frustration, hostility, and obstacles. He gradually built up in his mind a belief in obstruction and last-minute cancellations until a vicious circle had been established. What I fear most has come upon me. Mr Block realized that the trouble was in his mind, and that it was essential to change his mental attitude. His run of so-called misfortune was broken in the following way: 'I realize I am one with the infinite intelligence of my subconscious mind which knows no obstacle, difficulty, or delay. I live in the joyous expectancy of the best. My deeper mind responds to my thoughts. I know that the work of the infinite power of my subconscious cannot be hindered. Infinite intelligence always finishes successfully whatever it begins. Creative wisdom works through me bringing all my plans and purposes to completion. Whatever I start, I bring to a successful conclusion. My aim in life is to give wonderful service, and all those whom I contact are blessed by what I have to offer. All my work comes to full fruition in divine order.'

He repeated this prayer every morning before going to call on his customers, and he also prayed each night prior to sleep. In a short time he had established a new habit pattern in his subconscious mind, and he was back in his old accustomed stride as a successful salesman.

HOW MUCH DO YOU WANT WHAT YOU WANT?

A young man asked Socrates how he could get wisdom. Socrates replied, 'Come with me.' He took the lad to a river, pushed the boy's head under the water, held it there until the boy was gasping for air, then relaxed and released his head. When the boy regained his composure, he asked him, 'What did you desire most when you were under water?' 'I wanted air,' said the boy. Socrates said to him, 'When you want wisdom as much as you wanted air when you were immersed in the water, you will receive it.' Likewise, when you really have an intense desire to overcome any block in your life, and you come to a clear-cut decision that there is a way out, and that is the course you wish to follow, then victory and triumph are assured. If you really want peace of mind and inner calm, you will get it. Regardless of how unjustly you have been treated, or how unfair the boss has been, or what a mean scoundrel someone has proved to be, all this makes no difference to you when you awaken to your mental and spiritual powers. You know what you want, and you will definitely refuse to let the thieves (thoughts) of hatred, anger, hostility, and ill will rob you of peace, harmony, health, and happiness. You cease to become upset by people, conditions, news, and events by identifying your thoughts immediately with your aim in life. Your aim is peace, health, inspiration, harmony, and abundance. Feel a river of peace flowing through you now. Your thought is the immaterial and invisible power, and you choose to let it bless, inspire, and give you peace.

WHY HE COULD NOT BE HEALED

This is a case history of a married man with four children who was supporting and secretly living with another woman during his business trips. He was ill, nervous, irritable, and cantankerous, and he could not sleep without drugs. The doctor's medicine failed to bring down his high blood pressure of over two hundred. He had pains in numerous organs of his body, which doctors could not diagnose or relieve. To make matters worse, he was drinking heavily.

The cause of all this was a deep unconscious sense of guilt. He had violated the marriage vows, and this troubled him. The religious creed he was brought up on was deeply lodged in his subconscious mind, and he drank excessively to heal the wound of guilt. Some invalids take morphine and codeine for severe pains; he was taking alcohol for the pain or wound in his mind. It was the old story of adding fuel to the fire.

THE EXPLANATION AND THE CURE

He listened to the explanation of how his mind worked. He faced his problem, looked at it, and gave up his dual role. He knew that his drinking was an unconscious attempt to escape. The hidden cause lodged in his subconscious mind had to be eradicated; then the healing would follow. He began to impress his subconscious mind three or four times a day by using the following prayer: 'My mind is full of peace, poise, balance, and equilibrium. The infinite lies stretched in smiling repose within me. I am not afraid of anything in the past, the present, or the future. The infinite intelligence of my subconscious mind leads, guides, and directs me in all ways. I now meet every situation with faith, poise, calmness, and confidence. I am now completely free from the habit. My mind is full of inner peace, freedom, and joy. I forgive myself; then I am forgiven. Peace, sobriety, and confidence reign supreme in my mind.' He repeated this prayer frequently as outlined; being fully aware of what he was doing and why he was doing it. Knowing what he was doing gave him the necessary faith and confidence. I explained to him that as he spoke these statements out loud, slowly, lovingly, and meaningfully, they would gradually sink down into his subconscious mind. Like seeds, they would grow after their kind. These truths, on which he concentrated, went in through his eyes, his ears heard the sound, and the healing vibrations of these words reached his subconscious mind and obliterated all the negative mental patterns which caused all the trouble. Light dispels darkness. The constructive thought destroys the negative thought. He became a transformed man within a month.

REFUSING TO ADMIT IT

If you are an alcoholic or drug addict, admit it. Do not dodge the issue. Many people remain alcoholics because they refuse to admit it.

Your disease is instability, an inner fear. You are refusing to face life, and so you try to escape your responsibilities through the bottle. As an alcoholic you have no free will, although you think you have, and you may even boast about your will power. If you are a habitual drunkard and say bravely, 'I will not touch it anymore,' you have no power to make this assertion come true, because you do not know where to locate the power. You are living in a psychological prison of your own making, and you are bound by your beliefs, opinions, training, and environmental influences. Like most people, you are a creature of habit. You are conditioned to react the way you do.

BUILDING IN THE IDEA OF FREEDOM

You can build the idea of freedom and peace of mind into your mentality so that it reaches your subconscious depths. The latter, being all-powerful, will free you from all desire for alcohol. Then, you will have the new understanding of how your mind works, and you can truly back up your statement and prove the truth to yourself.

FIFTY-ONE PERCENT HEALED

If you have a keen desire to free yourself from any destructive habit, you are fifty-one percent healed already. When you have a greater desire to give up the bad habit than to continue it, you will not experience too much difficulty in gaining complete freedom. Whatever thought you anchor the mind upon, the latter magnifies. If you engage the mind on the concept of freedom (freedom from the habit) and peace of mind, and if you keep it focused on this new direction of attention, you generate feelings and emotions, which gradually emotionalize the concept of freedom and peace. Whatever idea you emotionalize is accepted by your subconscious and brought to pass.

SECTION III

SUCCESS AND WELL-BEING

.12.

Dale Carnegie

How to Win Friends and Influence People

Dale Carnegie describes how attentive listening makes one a good conversationalist.

~

AN EASY WAY TO BECOME A GOOD CONVERSATIONALIST

Some time ago, I attended a bridge party. I don't play bridge—and there was a woman there who didn't play bridge either. She had discovered that I had once been Lowell Thomas' manager before he went on the radio and that I had traveled in Europe a great deal while helping him prepare the illustrated travel talks he was then delivering. So she said: 'Oh, Mr Carnegie, I do want you to tell me about all the wonderful places you have visited and the sights you have seen.'

As we sat down on the sofa, she remarked that she and her husband had recently returned from a trip to Africa. 'Africa!' I exclaimed. 'How interesting! I've always wanted to see Africa, but I never got there except for a twenty-four-hour stay once in Algiers. Tell me, did you visit the big-game country? Yes? How fortunate. I envy you. Do tell me about Africa.'

That kept her talking for forty-five minutes. She never again asked me where I had been or what I had seen. She didn't want to hear me talk about my travels. All she wanted was an interested listener, so she could expand her ego and tell about where she had been.

Was she unusual? No. Many people are like that.

For example, I met a distinguished botanist at a dinner party given by a New York book publisher. I had never talked with a botanist before, and I found him fascinating. I literally sat on the edge of my chair and listened while he spoke of exotic plants and experiments in developing new forms of plant life and indoor gardens (and even told me astonishing facts about the humble potato). I had a small indoor garden of my own—and he was good enough to tell me how to solve some of my problems.

As I said, we were at a dinner party. There must have been a dozen other guests, but I violated all the canons of courtesy, ignored everyone else, and talked for hours to the botanist.

Midnight came, I said good night to everyone and departed. The botanist then turned to our host and paid me several flattering compliments. I was 'most stimulating.' I was this and I was that, and he ended by saying I was a 'most interesting conversationalist.'

An interesting conversationalist? Why, I had said hardly anything at all. I couldn't have said anything if I had wanted to without changing the subject, for I didn't know any more about botany than I knew about the anatomy of a penguin.

But I had done this: I had listened intently. I had listened because I was genuinely interested. And he felt it. Naturally that pleased him. That kind of listening is one of the highest compliments we can pay anyone. 'Few human beings,' wrote Jack Woodford in *Strangers in Love*, 'few human beings are proof against the implied flattery of rapt attention.' I went even further than giving him rapt attention. I was 'hearty in my approbation and lavish in my praise.'

I told him that I had been immensely entertained and instructed—and I had. I told him I wished I had his knowledge—and I did. I told him that I should love to wander the fields with him—and I have. I told him I must see him again—and I did.

And so I had him thinking of me as a good conversationalist when, in reality, I had been merely a good listener and had encouraged him to talk.

What is the secret, the mystery, of a successful business interview? Well, according to former Harvard president Charles W. Eliot, 'There is no mystery about successful business intercourse.... Exclusive attention to the person who is speaking to you is very important. Nothing else is so flattering as that.'

Eliot himself was a past master of the art of listening, Henry James, one of America's first great novelists, recalled: 'Dr Eliot's listening was not mere silence, but a form of activity. Sitting very erect on the end of his spine with hands joined in his lap, making no movement except that he revolved his thumbs around each other faster or slower, he faced his interlocutor and seemed to be hearing with his eyes as well as his ears. He listened with his mind and attentively considered what you had to say while you said it.... At the end of an interview the person who had talked to him felt that he had had his say.'

Self-evident, isn't it? You don't have to study for four years in Harvard to discover that. Yet I know and you know department store owners who will rent expensive space, buy their goods economically, dress their windows appealingly, spend thousands of dollars in advertising and then hire clerks who haven't the sense to be good listeners—clerks who interrupt customers, contradict them, irritate them, and all but drive them from the store.

A department store in Chicago almost lost a regular customer who spent several thousand dollars each year in that store because a sales clerk wouldn't listen. Mrs Henrietta Douglas, who took our course in Chicago, had purchased a coat at a special sale. After she had brought it home she noticed that there was a tear in the lining. She came back the next day and asked the sales clerk to exchange it. The clerk refused even to listen to her complaint. 'You bought this at a special sale,' she said. She pointed to a sign on the wall. 'Read that,' she exclaimed. 'All sales are final. Once you bought it, you have to keep it. Sew up the lining yourself.'

'But this was damaged merchandise,' Mrs Douglas complained.

'Makes no difference,' the clerk interrupted. 'Final's final.'

Mrs Douglas was about to walk out indignantly, swearing never to return to that store ever, when she was greeted by the department manager, who knew her from her many years of patronage. Mrs Douglas told her what had happened.

The manager listened attentively to the whole story,

examined the coat and then said: 'Special sales are "final" so we can dispose of merchandise at the end of the season. But this "no return" policy does not apply to damaged goods. We will certainly repair or replace the lining, or if you prefer, give you your money back.'

What a difference in treatment! If that manager had not come along and listened to the customer, a long-term patron of that store could have been lost forever.

Listening is just as important in one's home life as in the world of business. Millie Esposito of Croton-on-Hudson, New York, made it her business to listen carefully when one of her children wanted to speak with her. One evening she was sitting in the kitchen with her son, Robert, and after a brief discussion of something that was on his mind, Robert said: 'Mom, I know that you love me very much.'

Mrs Esposito was touched and said: 'Of course I love you very much. Did you doubt it?'

Robert responded: 'No, but I really know you love me because whenever I want to talk to you about something you stop whatever you are doing and listen to me.'

The chronic kicker, even the most violent critic, will frequently soften and be subdued in the presence of a patient, sympathetic listener—a listener who will be silent while the irate fault-finder dilates like a king cobra and spews the poison out of his system. To illustrate: the New York Telephone Company discovered a few years ago that it had to deal with one of the most vicious customers who ever cursed a customer service representative. And he did curse. He raved. He threatened to tear the phone out by its roots. He refused to pay certain charges that he declared were false.

He wrote letters to the newspapers. He filed innumerable complaints with the Public Service Commission, and he started several suits against the telephone company.

At last, one of the company's most skillful 'troubleshooters' was sent to interview this stormy petrel. This 'troubleshooter' listened and let the cantankerous customer enjoy himself pouring out his tirade. The telephone representative listened and said 'yes' and sympathized with his grievance.

'He raved on and I listened for nearly three hours,' the 'troubleshooter' said as he related his experiences before one of the author's classes. 'Then I went back and listened some more. I interviewed him four times, and before the fourth visit was over I had become a charter member of an organization he was starting. He called it the "Telephone Subscribers" Protective Association. I am still a member of this organization, and, so far as I know, I'm the only member in the world today besides Mr—.

'I listened and sympathized with him on every point that he made during these interviews. He had never had a telephone representative talk with him that way before, and he became almost friendly. The point on which I went to see him was not even mentioned on the first visit, nor was it mentioned on the second or third, but upon the fourth interview, I closed the case completely, he paid all his bills in full, and for the first time in the history of his difficulties with the telephone company he voluntarily withdrew his complaints from the Public Service Commission.'

Doubtless Mr— had considered himself a holy crusader, defending the public rights against callous exploitation. But in reality, what he had really wanted was a feeling of importance.

He got this feeling of importance at first by kicking and complaining. But as soon as he got his feeling of importance from a representative of the company, his imagined grievances vanished into thin air.

One morning years ago, an angry customer stormed into the office of Julian F. Detmer, founder of the Detmer Woolen Company, which later became the world's largest distributor of woolens to the tailoring trade.

'This man owed us a small sum of money,' Mr Detmer explained to me. 'The customer denied it, but we knew he was wrong. So our credit department had insisted that he pay. After getting a number of letters from our credit department, he packed his grip, made a trip to Chicago, and hurried into my office to inform me not only that he was not going to pay that bill, but that he was never going to buy another dollar's worth of goods from the Detmer Woolen Company.

'I listened patiently to all he had to say. I was tempted to interrupt, but I realized that would be bad policy, So I let him talk himself out. When he finally simmered down and got in a receptive mood, I said quietly: 'I want to thank you for coming to Chicago to tell me about this. You have done me a great favor, for if our credit department has annoyed you, it may annoy other good customers, and that would be just too bad. Believe me, I am far more eager to hear this than you are to tell it.'

'That was the last thing in the world he expected me to say. I think he was a trifle disappointed, because he had come to Chicago to tell me a thing or two, but here I was thanking him instead of scrapping with him. I assured him we would wipe the charge off the books and forget it, because he was a very careful man with only one account to look after, while our clerks had to look after thousands. Therefore, he was less likely to be wrong than we were.

'I told him that I understood exactly how he felt and that, if I were in his shoes, I should undoubtedly feel precisely as he did. Since he wasn't going to buy from us anymore, I recommended some other woolen houses.

'In the past, we had usually lunched together when he came to Chicago, so I invited him to have lunch with me this day. He accepted reluctantly, but when we came back to the office he placed a larger order than ever before. He returned home in a softened mood and, wanting to be just as fair with us as we had been with him, looked over his bills, found one that had been mislaid, and sent us a check with his apologies.

'Later, when his wife presented him with a baby boy, he gave his son the middle name of Detmer, and he remained a friend and customer of the house until his death twenty-two years afterwards.'

Years ago, a poor Dutch immigrant boy washed the windows of a bakery shop after school to help support his family. His people were so poor that in addition he used to go out in the street with a basket every day and collect stray bits of coal that had fallen in the gutter where the coal wagons had delivered fuel. That boy, Edward Bok, never got more than six years of schooling in his life; yet eventually he made himself one of the most successful magazine editors in the history of American journalism. How did he do it? That is a long story, but how he got his start can be told briefly. He got his start by using the principles advocated in this chapter.

He left school when he was thirteen and became an office boy for Western Union, but he didn't for one moment give up the idea of an education. Instead, he started to educate himself. He saved his carfares and went without lunch until he had enough money to buy an encyclopedia of American biography—and then he did an unheard-of thing. He read the lives of famous people and wrote them asking for additional information about their childhoods. He was a good listener. He asked famous people to tell him more about themselves. He wrote General James A. Garfield, who was then running for President, and asked if it was true that he was once a tow boy on a canal; and Garfield replied. He wrote General Grant asking about a certain battle, and Grant drew a map for him and invited this fourteen-year-old boy to dinner and spent the evening talking to him.

Soon our Western Union messenger boy was corresponding with many of the most famous people in the nation: Ralph Waldo Emerson, Oliver Wendell Holmes, Longfellow, Mrs Abraham Lincoln, Louisa May Alcott, General Sherman, and Jefferson Davis. Not only did he correspond with these distinguished people, but as soon as he got a vacation, he visited many of them as a welcome guest in their homes. This experience imbued him with a confidence that was invaluable. These men and women fired him with a vision and ambition that shaped his life. And all this, let me repeat, was made possible solely by the application of the principles we are discussing here.

Isaac F. Marcosson, a journalist who interviewed hundreds

of celebrities, declared that many people fail to make a favorable impression because they don't listen attentively. 'They have been so much concerned with what they are going to say next that they do not keep their ears open.... Very important people have told me that they prefer good listeners to good talkers, but the ability to listen seems rarer than almost any other good trait.'

And not only important personages crave a good listener, but ordinary folk do too. As the Reader's Digest once said: 'Many persons call a doctor when all they want is an audience.'

During the darkest hours of the Civil War, Lincoln wrote to an old friend in Springfield, Illinois, asking him to come to Washington. Lincoln said he had some problems he wanted to discuss with him. The old neighbor called at the White House, and Lincoln talked to him for hours about the advisability of issuing a proclamation freeing the slaves. Lincoln went over all the arguments for and against such a move, and then read letters and newspaper articles, some denouncing him for not freeing the slaves and others denouncing him for fear he was going to free them. After talking for hours, Lincoln shook hands with his old neighbor, said good night, and sent him back to Illinois without even asking for his opinion. Lincoln had done all the talking himself. That seemed to clarify his mind. 'He seemed to feel easier after that talk,' the old friend said. Lincoln hadn't wanted advice, he had wanted merely a friendly, sympathetic listener to whom he could unburden himself. That's what we all want when we are in trouble. That is frequently all the irritated customer wants, and the dissatisfied employee or the hurt friend.

One of the great listeners of modern times was Sigmund Freud. A man who met Freud described his manner of listening: 'It struck me so forcibly that I shall never forget him. He had qualities which I had never seen in any other man. Never had I seen such concentrated attention. There was none of that piercing 'soul penetrating gaze' business. His eyes were mild and genial. His voice was low and kind. His gestures were few. But the attention he gave me, his appreciation of what I said, even when I said it badly, was extraordinary. *You've no idea what it meant to be listened to like that.*'

If you want to know how to make people shun you and laugh at you behind your back and even despise you, here is the recipe: never listen to anyone for long. Talk incessantly about yourself. If you have an idea while the other person is talking, don't wait for him or her to finish: bust right in and interrupt in the middle of a sentence.

Do you know people like that? I do, unfortunately; and the astonishing part of it is that some of them are prominent.

Bores, that is all they are—bores intoxicated with their own egos, drunk with a sense of their own importance.

People who talk only of themselves think only of themselves. And 'those people who think only of themselves,' Dr Nicholas Murray Butler, longtime president of Columbia University, said, 'are hopelessly uneducated. They are not educated,' said Dr Butler, 'no matter how instructed they may be.'

So if you aspire to be a good conversationalist, be an attentive listener. To be interesting, be interested. Ask questions that other persons will enjoy answering. Encourage them to talk about themselves and their accomplishments. Remember that the people you are talking to are a hundred times more interested in themselves and their wants and problems than they are in you and your problems. A person's toothache means more to that person than a famine in China which kills a million people. A boil on one's neck interests one more than forty earthquakes in Africa. Think of that the next time you start a conversation.

.13.

His Holiness the Dalai Lama

Countering Stress and Depression

His Holiness the Dalai Lama teaches the reader how to transform the mind to achieve happiness and success.

~

At a fundamental level, as human beings, we are all the same; each one of us aspires to happiness and each one of us does not wish to suffer. This is why, whenever I have the opportunity, I try to draw people's attention to what as members of the human family we have in common and the deeply interconnected nature of our existence and welfare.

Today, there is increasing recognition, as well as a growing body of scientific evidence, that confirms the close connection between our own states of mind and our happiness. On the one hand, many of us live in societies that are very developed materially, yet among us are many people who are not very happy. Just underneath the beautiful surface of affluence there is a kind of mental unrest, leading to frustration, unnecessary quarrels, reliance on drugs or alcohol, and in the worst case, suicide. There is no guarantee that wealth alone can give you the joy or fulfilment that you seek. The same can be said of your friends too. When you are in an intense state of anger or hatred, even a very close friend appears to you as somehow frosty, or cold, distant, and annoying.

However, as human beings we are gifted with this wonderful human intelligence. Besides that, all human beings have the capacity to be very determined and to direct that strong sense of determination in whatever direction they like. So long as we remember that we have this marvellous gift of human intelligence and a capacity to develop determination and use it in positive ways, we will preserve our underlying mental health. Realizing we have this great human potential gives us a fundamental strength. This recognition can act as a mechanism that enables us to deal with any difficulty, no matter what situation we are facing, without losing hope or sinking into feelings of low self-esteem.

I write this as someone who lost his freedom at the age of sixteen, then lost his country at the age of twenty-four. Consequently, I have lived in exile for more than fifty years during which we Tibetans have dedicated ourselves to keeping the Tibetan identity alive and preserving our culture and values. On most days the news from Tibet is heartbreaking, and yet none of these challenges are grounds for giving up. One of the approaches that I personally find useful is to cultivate the thought: if the situation or problem is such that it can be remedied, then there is no need to worry about it. In other words, if there is a solution or a way out of the difficulty, you do not need to be overwhelmed by it. The appropriate action is to seek its solution. Then it is clearly more sensible to spend your energy focussing on the solution rather than worrying about the problem. Alternatively, if there is no solution, no possibility of resolution, then there is also no point in being worried about it, because you cannot do anything about it anyway. In that case, the sooner you accept this fact, the easier it will be for you. This formula, of course, implies directly confronting the problem and taking a realistic view. Otherwise you will be unable to find out whether or not there is a resolution to the problem.

Taking a realistic view and cultivating a proper motivation can also shield you against feelings of fear and anxiety. If you develop a pure and sincere motivation, if you are motivated by a wish to help on the basis of kindness, compassion, and respect, then you can carry on any kind of work, in any field, and function more effectively with less fear or worry, not being afraid of what others think or whether you ultimately will be successful in reaching your goal. Even if you fail to achieve your goal, you can feel good about having made the effort. But with a bad motivation, people can praise you or you can achieve goals, but you still will not be happy.

Again, we may sometimes feel that our whole lives are unsatisfactory, we feel on the point of being overwhelmed by the difficulties that confront us. This happens to us all in varying degrees from time to time. When this occurs, it is vital that we make every effort to find a way of lifting our spirits. We can do this by recollecting our good fortune. We may, for example, be loved by someone; we may have certain talents; we may have received a good education; we may have our basic needs provided for—food to eat, clothes to wear, somewhere to live—we may have performed certain altruistic deeds in the past. We must take into consideration even the slightest positive aspect of our lives. For if we fail to find some way of uplifting ourselves, there is every danger of sinking further into our sense of powerlessness. This can lead us to believe that we have no capacity for doing good whatsoever. Thus we create the conditions of despair itself.

As a Buddhist monk I have learned that what principally upsets our inner peace is what we call disturbing emotions. All those thoughts, emotions, and mental events which reflect a negative or uncompassionate state of mind inevitably undermine our experience of inner peace. All our negative thoughts and emotions—such as hatred, anger, pride, lust, greed, envy, and so on—are considered to be sources of difficulty, to be disturbing. Negative thoughts and emotions are what obstruct our most basic aspiration—to be happy and to avoid suffering. When we act under their influence, we become oblivious to the impact our actions have on others: they are thus the cause of our destructive behaviour both towards others and to ourselves. Murder, scandal, and deceit all have their origin in disturbing emotions.

This inevitably gives rise to the question—can we train the mind? There are many methods by which to do this. Among these, in the Buddhist tradition, is a special instruction called mind training, which focuses on cultivating concern for others and turning adversity to advantage. It is this pattern of thought, transforming problems into happiness that has enabled the Tibetan people to maintain their dignity and spirit in the face of great difficulties. Indeed I have found this advice of great practical benefit in my own life.

A great Tibetan teacher of mind training once remarked that one of the mind's most marvellous qualities is that it can be transformed. I have no doubt that those who attempt to transform their minds, overcome their disturbing emotions and achieve a sense of inner peace, will, over a period of time, notice a change in their mental attitudes and responses to people and events. Their minds will become more disciplined and positive. And I am sure they will find their own sense of happiness grow as they contribute to the greater happiness of others. I offer my prayers that everyone who makes this their goal will be blessed with success.

.14.

Joseph Murphy

The Power of Your Subconscious Mind

Joseph Murphy provides numerous tips on banishing fear.

~

HOW TO USE YOUR SUBCONSCIOUS MIND TO REMOVE FEAR

One of our students told me that he was invited to speak at a banquet. He said he was panic-stricken at the thought of speaking before a thousand people. He overcame his fear this way: for several nights he sat down in an armchair for about five minutes and said to himself slowly, quietly, and positively, 'I am going to master this fear. I am overcoming it now. I speak with poise and confidence. I am relaxed and at ease.' He operated a definite law of mind and overcame his fear. The subconscious mind is amenable to suggestion and is controlled by suggestion. When you still your mind and relax, the thoughts of your conscious mind sink down into the subconscious through a process similar to osmosis, whereby fluids separated by a porous membrane intermingle. As these positive seeds, or thoughts, sink into the subconscious area, they grow after their kind, and you become poised, serene, and calm.

MAN'S GREATEST ENEMY

It is said that fear is man's greatest enemy. Fear is behind failure, sickness, and poor human relations. Millions of people are afraid of the past, the future, old age, insanity, and death. Fear is a thought in your mind, and you are afraid of your own thoughts. A little boy can be paralyzed with fear when he is told there is a boogieman under his bed that is going to take him away. When his father turns on the light and shows him there is no boogieman, he is freed from fear. The fear in the mind of the boy was as real as if there really was a boogieman there. He was healed of a false thought in his mind. The thing he feared did not exist. Likewise, most of your fears have no reality. They are merely a conglomeration of sinister shadows and shadows have no reality.

DO THE THING YOU FEAR

Ralph Waldo Emerson, philosopher and poet, said, 'Do the thing you are afraid to do, and the death of fear is certain.'

There was a time when the writer of this chapter was filled with unutterable fear when standing before an audience. The way I overcame it was to stand before the audience, do the thing I was afraid to do, and the death of fear was certain. When you affirm positively that you are going to master your fears, and you come to a definite decision in your conscious mind, you release the power of the subconscious, which flows in response to the nature of your thought.

BANISHING STAGE FRIGHT

A young lady was invited to an audition. She had been looking forward to the interview. However, on three previous occasions, she had failed miserably due to stage fright. She possessed a very good voice, but she was certain that when the time came for her to sing, she would be seized with stage fright. The subconscious mind takes your fears as a request, proceeds to manifest them, and brings them into your experience. On three previous auditions she sang wrong notes, and she finally broke down and cried. The cause, as previously outlined, was an involuntary autosuggestion, i.e., a silent fear thought emotionalized and subjectified. She overcame it by the following technique: three times a day she isolated herself in a room. She sat down comfortably in an armchair, relaxed her body, and closed her eyes. She stilled her mind and body to the best of her ability. Physical inertia favours passivity and renders the mind more receptive to suggestion. She counteracted the fear suggestion by its converse, saying to herself, 'I sing beautifully. I am poised, serene, confident, and calm.' She repeated the words slowly, quietly, and with feeling from five to ten times at each sitting. She had three such 'sittings' every day and one immediately prior to sleep at night. At the end of a week she was completely poised and confident, and gave a definitely outstanding audition. Carry out the above procedure, and the death of fear is certain.

FEAR OF FAILURE

Occasionally young men from the local university come to see me, as well as schoolteachers, who often seem to suffer from suggestive amnesia at examinations. The complaint is always the same: 'I know the answers after the examination is over, but I can't remember the answers during the examination.' The idea, which realizes itself, is the one to which we invariably give concentrated attention. I find that each one is obsessed with the idea of failure. Fear is behind the temporary amnesia, and it is the cause of the whole experience. One young medical student was the most brilliant person in his class, yet he found himself failing to answer simple questions at the time of written or oral examinations. I explained to him that the reason was he had been worrying and was fearful for several days previous to the examination. These negative thoughts became charged with fear. Thoughts enveloped in the powerful emotion of fear are realized in the subconscious mind. In other words, this young man was requesting his subconscious mind to see to it that he failed, and that is exactly what it did. On the day of the examination he found himself stricken with what is called, in psychological circles, suggestive amnesia.

HOW HE OVERCAME THE FEAR

He learned that his subconscious mind was the storehouse of memory, and that it had a perfect record of all he had heard and read during his medical training. Moreover, he learned that the subconscious mind was responsive and reciprocal. The way to be en rapport with it was to be relaxed, peaceful, and confident. Every night and morning he began to imagine his mother congratulating him on his wonderful record. He would hold an imaginary letter from her in his hand. As he began to contemplate the happy result, he called forth a corresponding or reciprocal response or reaction in himself. The all-wise and omnipotent power of the subconscious took over, dictated, and directed his conscious mind accordingly. He imagined the end, thereby willing the means to the realization of the end. Following this procedure, he had no trouble passing subsequent examinations. In other words, the subjective wisdom took over, compelling him to give an excellent account of himself.

FEAR OF WATER, MOUNTAINS, CLOSED PLACES, ETC.

There are many people who are afraid to go into an elevator, climb mountains, or even swim in the water. It may well be that the individual had unpleasant experiences in the water in his youth, such as having been thrown forcibly into the water without being able to swim. He might have been forcibly detained in an elevator, which failed to function properly, causing resultant fear of closed places. I had an experience when I was about ten years of age. I accidentally fell into a pool and went down three times. I can still remember the dark water engulfing my head, and my gasping for air until another boy pulled me out at the last moment. This experience sank into my subconscious mind, and for years I feared the water. An elderly psychologist said to me, 'Go down to the swimming pool, look at the water, and say out loud in strong tones, "I am going to master you. I can dominate you." Then go into the water, take lessons, and overcome it.' This I did, and I mastered the water. Do not permit water to master you. Remember, you are the master of the water. When I assumed a new attitude of mind, the omnipotent power of the subconscious responded, giving me strength, faith, and confidence, and enabling me to overcome my fear.

MASTER TECHNIQUE FOR OVERCOMING ANY PARTICULAR FEAR

The following is a process and technique for overcoming fear, which I teach from the platform. It works like a charm. Try it! Suppose you are afraid of the water, a mountain, an interview, an audition, or you fear closed places. If you are afraid of swimming, begin now to sit still for five or ten minutes three or four times a day, and imagine you are swimming. Actually, you are swimming in your mind. It is a subjective experience. Mentally you have projected yourself into the water. You feel the chill of the water and the movement of your arms and legs. It is all real, vivid, and a joyous activity of the mind. It is not idle daydreaming, for you know that what you are experiencing in your imagination will be developed in your subconscious mind. Then you will be compelled to express the image and likeness of the picture you impressed on your deeper mind. This is the law of the subconscious. You could apply the same technique if you are afraid of mountains or high places. Imagine you are climbing the mountain, feel the reality of it all, enjoy the scenery, knowing that as you continue to do this mentally, you will do it physically with ease and comfort.

HE BLESSED THE ELEVATOR

I knew an executive of a large corporation who was terrified to ride in an elevator. He would walk up five flights of stairs to his office every morning. He said that he began to bless the elevator every night and several times a day. He finally overcame his fear. This was how he blessed the elevator: 'The elevator in our building is a wonderful idea. It came out of the universal mind. It is a boon and a blessing to all our employees. It gives wonderful service. It operates in divine order. I ride in it in peace and joy. I remain silent now while the currents of life, love, and understanding flow through the patterns of my thought. In my imagination I am now in the elevator, and I step out into my office. The elevator is full of our employees. I talk to them, and they are friendly, joyous, and free. It is a wonderful experience of freedom, faith, and confidence. I give thanks.' He continued this prayer for about ten days, and on the eleventh day, he walked into the elevator with other members of the organization and felt completely free.

NORMAL AND ABNORMAL FEAR

Man is born only with two fears, the fear of falling and the fear of noise. These are an alarm system given you by nature as a means of self-preservation. Normal fear is good. You hear an automobile coming down the road, and you step aside to survive. The momentary fear of being run over is overcome by your action. All other fears were given to you by parents, relatives, teachers, and all those who influenced your early years.

ABNORMAL FEAR

Abnormal fear takes place when man lets his imagination run riot. I knew a woman who was invited to go on a trip around the world by plane. She began to cut out of the newspapers all reports of airplane catastrophes. She pictured herself going down in the ocean, being drowned, etc. This is abnormal fear. Had she persisted in this, she would undoubtedly have attracted what she feared most.

Another example of abnormal fear is that of a businessman in New York, who was very prosperous and successful. He had his own private mental motion picture of which he was the director. He would run this mental movie of failure, bankruptcy, empty shelves, and no bank balance until he sank into a deep depression. He refused to stop this morbid imagery and kept reminding his wife that 'this can't last,' 'there will be a recession,' 'I feel sure we will go bankrupt,' etc. His wife told me that he finally did go into bankruptcy, and all the things he imagined and feared came to pass. The things he feared did not exist, but he brought them to pass by constantly fearing, believing, and expecting financial disaster. Job said, the thing I feared has come upon me. There are people who are afraid that something terrible will happen to their children, and that some dreaded catastrophe will befall them. When they read about an epidemic or rare disease, they live in fear that they will catch it, and some imagine they have the disease already. All this is abnormal fear.

THE ANSWER TO ABNORMAL FEAR

Move mentally to the opposite. To stay at the extreme of fear is stagnation plus mental and physical deterioration. When fear arises, there immediately comes with it a desire for something opposite to the thing feared. Place your attention on the thing immediately desired. Get absorbed and engrossed in your desire, knowing that the subjective always overturns the objective. This attitude will give you confidence and lift your spirits. The infinite power of your subconscious mind is moving on your behalf, and it cannot fail. Therefore, peace and assurance are yours.

EXAMINE YOUR FEARS

The president of a large organization told me that when he was a salesman he used to walk around the block five or six times before he called on a customer. The sales manager came along one day and said to him 'Don't be afraid of the boogieman behind the door. There is no boogieman. It is a false belief.' The manager told him that whenever he looked at his own fears he stared them in the face and stood up to them, looking them straight in the eye. Then they faded and shrank into insignificance.

HE LANDED IN THE JUNGLE

A chaplain told me of his experiences in the Second World War. He had to parachute from a damaged plane and land in the jungle. He said he was frightened, but he knew there were two kinds of fear, normal and abnormal, which we have previously pointed out. He decided to do something about the fear immediately and began to talk to himself saying, 'John, you can't surrender to your fear. Your fear is a desire for safety and security, and a way out.' He began to claim; 'Infinite intelligence which guides the planets in their courses is now leading and guiding me out of this jungle.' He kept saying this out loud to himself for ten minutes or more. 'Then,' he added, 'Something began to stir inside me. A mood of confidence began to seize me, and I began to walk. After a few days, I miraculously came out of the jungle, and was picked up by a rescue plane.' His changed mental attitude saved him. His confidence and trust in the subjective wisdom and power within him was the solution to his problem. He said, 'Had I begun to bemoan my fate and indulge my fears, I would have succumbed to the monster fear, and probably would have died of fear and starvation.'

HE DISMISSED HIMSELF

The general manager of an organization told me that for three years he feared he would lose his position. He was always imagining failure. The thing he feared did not exist, save as a morbid anxious thought in his own mind. His vivid imagination dramatized the loss of his job until he became nervous and neurotic. Finally he was asked to resign. Actually, he dismissed himself. His constant negative imagery and fear suggestions to his subconscious mind caused the latter to respond and react accordingly. It caused him to make mistakes and foolish decisions, which resulted in his failure as a general manager. His dismissal would never have happened, if he had immediately moved to the opposite in his mind.

THEY PLOTTED AGAINST HIM

During a recent world lecture tour, I had a two-hour conversation with a prominent government official. He had a deep sense of inner peace and serenity. He said that all the abuse he receives politically from newspapers and the opposition party never disturb him. His practice is to sit still for fifteen minutes in the morning and realize that in the centre of him is a deep still ocean of peace. Meditating in this way, he generates tremendous power, which overcomes all manner of difficulties and fears. Some time previously, a colleague called him at midnight and told him a group of people was plotting against him. This is what he said to his colleague, 'I am going to sleep now in perfect peace. You can discuss it with me at 10:00 A.M. tomorrow.' He said to me, 'I know that no negative thought can ever manifest except I emotionalize the thought and accept it mentally. I refuse to entertain their suggestion of fear. Therefore, no harm can come to me.' Notice how calm he was, how cool, how peaceful! He did not start getting excited, tearing his hair, or wringing his hands. At his centre he found the still water, an inner peace, and there was a great calm.

DELIVER YOURSELF FROM ALL YOUR FEARS

Use this perfect formula for casting out fear. 'I sought the Lord, and He heard me, and delivered me from all my fears.' PSALM 34:4. The Lord is an ancient word meaning law—the power of your subconscious mind. Learn the wonders of your subconscious, and how it works and functions. Master the techniques given to you in this chapter. Put them into practice now, today! Your subconscious will respond, and you will be free of all fears. I sought the Lord, and He heard me, and delivered me from all my fears.

.15.

Napoleon Hill

Think and Grow Rich

Here, Napoleon Hill reveals how to master procrastination.

~

THE MASTERY OF PROCRASTINATION

ACCURATE analysis of over 25,000 men and women who had experienced failure, disclosed the fact that LACK OF DECISION was near the head of the list of the thirty major causes of FAILURE. This is no mere statement of a theory—it is a fact.

PROCRASTINATION, the opposite of DECISION, is a common enemy which practically every man must conquer....

Analysis of several hundred people who had accumulated fortunes well beyond the million dollar mark, disclosed the fact that every one of them had the habit of REACHING DECISIONS PROMPTLY, and of changing these decisions SLOWLY, if, and when they were changed. People who fail to accumulate money, without exception, have the habit of reaching decisions, IF AT ALL, very slowly, and of changing these decisions quickly and often.

One of Henry Ford's most outstanding qualities is his habit of reaching decisions quickly and definitely, and changing them slowly. This quality is so pronounced in Mr Ford, that it has given him the reputation of being obstinate. It was this quality which prompted Mr Ford to continue to manufacture his famous Model 'T' (the world's ugliest car), when all of his advisors, and many of the purchasers of the car, were urging him to change it.

Perhaps, Mr Ford delayed too long in making the change, but the other side of the story is, that Mr Ford's firmness of decision yielded a huge fortune, before the change in model became necessary. There is but little doubt that Mr Ford's habit of definiteness of decision assumes the proportion of obstinacy, but this quality is preferable to slowness in reaching decisions and quickness in changing them.

The majority of people who fail to accumulate money sufficient for their needs, are, generally, easily influenced by the 'opinions' of others. They permit the newspapers and the 'gossiping' neighbors to do their 'thinking' for them. Opinions are the cheapest commodities on earth. Everyone has a flock of opinions ready to be wished upon anyone who will accept them. If you are influenced by 'opinions' when you reach DECISIONS, you will not succeed in any undertaking, much less in that of transmuting YOUR OWN DESIRE into money.

If you are influenced by the opinions of others, you will have no DESIRE of your own.

Keep your own counsel, when you begin to put into practice the principles described here, by reaching your own decisions and following them....

Close friends and relatives, while not meaning to do so, often handicap one through 'opinions' and sometimes through ridicule, which is meant to be humorous. Thousands of men and women carry inferiority complexes with them all through life, because some well-meaning, but ignorant person destroyed their confidence through 'opinions' or ridicule.

You have a brain and mind of your own. USE IT, and reach your own decisions. If you need facts or information from other people, to enable you to reach decisions, as you probably will in many instances; acquire these facts or secure the information you need quietly, without disclosing your purpose.

It is characteristic of people who have but a smattering or a veneer of knowledge to try to give the impression that they have much knowledge. Such people generally do TOO MUCH talking and TOO LITTLE listening. Keep your eyes and ears wide open—and your mouth CLOSED, if you wish to acquire the habit of prompt DECISION. Those who talk too much do little else. If you talk more than you listen, you not only deprive yourself of many opportunities to accumulate useful knowledge, but you also disclose your PLANS and PURPOSES to people who will take great delight in defeating you, because they envy you. Remember, also, that every time you open your mouth in the presence of a person who has an abundance of knowledge, you display to that person, your exact stock of knowledge, or your LACK of it! Genuine wisdom is usually conspicuous through modesty and silence.

Keep in mind the fact that every person with whom you associate is, like yourself, seeking the opportunity to accumulate money. If you talk about your plans too freely, you may be surprised when you learn that some other person has beaten you to your goal by PUTTING INTO ACTION AHEAD OF YOU, the plans of which you talked unwisely.

Let one of your first decisions be to KEEP A CLOSED MOUTH AND OPEN EARS AND EYES.

As a reminder to yourself to follow this advice, it will be helpful if you copy the following epigram in large letters and place it where you will see it daily.

'TELL THE WORLD WHAT YOU INTEND TO DO, BUT FIRST SHOW IT.'

This is the equivalent of saying that 'deeds, and not words, are what count most.'

.16.

James Allen

As a Man Thinketh

James Allen details how to cultivate good thoughts for good results and well-being.

~

EFFECT OF THOUGHT ON CIRCUMSTANCES

Man's mind may be likened to a garden, which may be intelligently cultivated or allowed to run wild; but whether cultivated or neglected, it must, and will, bring forth. If no useful seeds are put into it, then an abundance of useless weed-seeds will fall therein, and will continue to produce their kind.

Just as a gardener cultivates his plot, keeping it free from weeds, and growing the flowers and fruits which he requires, so may a man tend the garden of his mind, weeding out all the wrong, useless, and impure thoughts, and cultivating toward perfection the flowers and fruits of right, useful, and pure thoughts. By pursuing this process, a man sooner or later discovers that he is the master-gardener of his soul, the director of his life.

He also reveals, within himself, the laws of thought, and understands, with ever-increasing accuracy, how the thought-forces and mind elements operate in the shaping of his character, circumstances, and destiny.

Thought and character are one, and as character can only manifest and discover itself through environment and circumstance, the outer conditions of a person's life will always be found to be harmoniously related to his inner state. This does not mean that a man's circumstances at any given time are an indication of his entire character, but that those circumstances are so intimately connected with some vital thought-element within himself that, for the time being, they are indispensable to his development.

Every man is where he is by the law of his being; the thoughts which he has built into his character have brought him there, and in the arrangement of his life there is no element of chance, but all is the result of a law which cannot err. This is just as true of those who feel 'out of harmony' with their surroundings as of those who are contented with them.

As a progressive and evolving being, man is where he is that he may learn that he may grow; and as he learns the spiritual lesson which any circumstance contains for him, it passes away and gives place to other circumstances.

Man is buffeted by circumstances so long as he believes himself to be the creature of outside conditions, but when he realizes that he is a creative power, and that he may command the hidden soil and seeds of his being out of which circumstances grow, he then becomes the rightful master of himself.

That circumstances grow out of thought every man knows who has for any length of time practised self-control and self-purification, for he will have noticed that the alteration in his circumstances has been in exact ratio with his altered mental condition. So true is this that when a man earnestly applies himself to remedy the defects in his character, and makes swift and marked progress, he passes rapidly through a succession of vicissitudes.

The soul attracts that which it secretly harbours; that which it loves, and also that which it fears; it reaches the height of its cherished aspirations; it falls to the level of its unchastened desires—and circumstances are the means by which the soul receives its own.

Every thought-seed sown or allowed to fall into the mind, and to take root there, produces its own, blossoming sooner or later into act, and bearing its own fruitage of opportunity and circumstance. Good thoughts bear good fruit, bad thoughts bad fruit.

The outer world of circumstance shapes itself to the inner world of thought, and both pleasant and unpleasant external conditions are factors, which make for the ultimate good of the individual. As the reaper of his own harvest, man learns both by suffering and bliss.

Following the inmost desires, aspirations, thoughts, by which he allows himself to be dominated, (pursuing the will-o'-the-wisps of impure imaginings or steadfastly walking the highway of strong and high endeavour), a man at last arrives at their fruition and fulfilment in the outer conditions of his life. The laws of growth and adjustment everywhere obtains.

A man does not come to the almshouse or the jail by the tyranny of fate or circumstance, but by the pathway of grovelling thoughts and base desires. Nor does a pure-minded man fall suddenly into crime by stress of any mere external force; the criminal thought had long been secretly fostered in the heart, and the hour of opportunity revealed its gathered power. Circumstance does not make the man; it reveals him to himself. No such conditions can exist as descending into vice and its attendant sufferings apart from vicious inclinations, or ascending into virtue and its pure happiness without the continued cultivation of virtuous aspirations; and man, therefore, as the lord and master of thought, is the maker of himself the shaper and author of environment. Even at birth the soul comes to its own and through every step of its earthly pilgrimage it attracts those combinations of conditions which reveal itself, which are the reflections of its own purity and, impurity, its strength and weakness.

Men do not attract that which they want, but that which they are. Their whims, fancies, and ambitions are thwarted at every step, but their inmost thoughts and desires are fed with their own food, be it foul or clean. The 'divinity that shapes our ends' is in ourselves; it is our very self. Only himself manacles man: thought and action are the gaolers of Fate—they imprison, being base; they are also the angels of Freedom—they liberate, being noble. Not what he wishes and prays for does a man get, but what he justly earns. His wishes and prayers are only gratified and answered when they harmonize with his thoughts and actions.

In the light of this truth, what, then, is the meaning of 'fighting against circumstances?' It means that a man is continually revolting against an effect without, while all the time he is nourishing and preserving its cause in his heart. That cause may take the form of a conscious vice or an unconscious weakness; but whatever it is, it stubbornly retards the efforts of its possessor, and thus calls aloud for remedy.

Men are anxious to improve their circumstances, but are unwilling to improve themselves; they therefore remain bound. The man who does not shrink from self-crucifixion can never fail to accomplish the object upon which his heart is set. This is as true of earthly as of heavenly things. Even the man whose sole object is to acquire wealth must be prepared to make great personal sacrifices before he can accomplish his object; and how much more so he who would realize a strong and well-poised life?

Here is a man who is wretchedly poor. He is extremely anxious that his surroundings and home comforts should be improved, yet all the time he shirks his work, and considers he is justified in trying to deceive his employer on the ground of the insufficiency of his wages. Such a man does not understand the simplest rudiments of those principles which are the basis of true prosperity, and is not only totally unfitted to rise out of his wretchedness, but is actually attracting to himself a still deeper wretchedness by dwelling in, and acting out, indolent, deceptive, and unmanly thoughts.

Here is a rich man who is the victim of a painful and persistent disease as the result of gluttony. He is willing to give large sums of money to get rid of it, but he will not sacrifice his gluttonous desires. He wants to gratify his taste for rich and unnatural viands and have his health as well. Such a man is totally unfit to have health, because he has not yet learned the first principles of a healthy life.

Here is an employer of labour who adopts crooked measures to avoid paying the regulation wage, and, in the hope of making larger profits, reduces the wages of his work people. Such a man is altogether unfitted for prosperity, and when he finds himself bankrupt, both as regards reputation and riches, he blames circumstances, not knowing that he is the sole author of his condition.

I have introduced these three cases merely as illustrative of the truth that man is the causer (though nearly always is unconsciously) of his circumstances, and that, whilst aiming at a good end, he is continually frustrating its accomplishment by encouraging thoughts and desires which cannot possibly harmonize with that end. Such cases could be multiplied and varied almost indefinitely, but this is not necessary, as the reader can, if he so resolves, trace the action of the laws of thought in his own mind and life, and until this is done, mere external facts cannot serve as a ground of reasoning.

Circumstances, however, are so complicated, thought is so deeply rooted, and the conditions of happiness vary so vastly with individuals, that a man's entire soul-condition (although it may be known to himself) cannot be judged by another from the external aspect of his life alone. A man may be honest in certain directions, yet suffer privations; a man may be dishonest in certain directions, yet acquire wealth; but the conclusion usually formed that the one man fails because of his particular honesty, and that the other prospers because of his particular dishonesty, is the result of a superficial judgement, which assumes that the dishonest man is almost totally corrupt, and the honest man almost entirely virtuous.

In the light of a deeper knowledge and wider experience such judgement is found to be erroneous. The dishonest man may have some admirable virtues, which the other does, not possess; and the honest man obnoxious vices which are absent in the other. The honest man reaps the good results of his honest thoughts and acts; he also brings upon himself the sufferings, which his vices produce. The dishonest man likewise garners his own suffering and happiness.

It is pleasing to human vanity to believe that one suffers because of one's virtue; but not until a man has extirpated every sickly, bitter, and impure thought from his mind, and washed every sinful stain from his soul, can he be in a position to know and declare that his sufferings are the result of his good, and not of his bad qualities; and on the way to, yet long before he has reached, that supreme perfection, he will have found, working in his mind and life, the Great Law which is absolutely just, and which cannot, therefore, give good for evil, evil for good. Possessed of such knowledge, he will then know, looking back upon his past ignorance and blindness, that his life is, and always was, justly ordered, and that all his past experiences, good and bad, were the equitable outworking of his evolving, yet unevolved self.

Good thoughts and actions can never produce bad results; bad thoughts and actions can never produce good results. This is but saying that nothing can come from corn but corn, nothing from nettles but nettles. Men understand this law in the natural world, and work with it; but few understand it in the mental and moral world (though its operation there is just as simple and undeviating), and they, therefore, do not co-operate with it.

Suffering is always the effect of wrong thought in some direction. It is an indication that the individual is out of harmony with himself, with the Law of his being. The sole and supreme use of suffering is to purify, to burn out all that is useless and impure. Suffering ceases for him who is pure. There could be no object in burning gold after the dross had been removed, and a perfectly pure and enlightened being could not suffer.

The circumstances, which a man encounters with suffering, are the result of his own mental in harmony. The circumstances, which a man encounters with blessedness, are the result of his own mental harmony. Blessedness, not material possessions, is the measure of right thought; wretchedness, not lack of material possessions, is the measure of wrong thought. A man may be cursed and rich; he may be blessed and poor. Blessedness and riches are only joined together when the riches are rightly and wisely used; and the poor man only descends into wretchedness when he regards his lot as a burden unjustly imposed.

Indigence and indulgence are the two extremes of wretchedness. They are both equally unnatural and the result of mental disorder. A man is not rightly conditioned until he is a happy, healthy, and prosperous being; and happiness, health, and prosperity are the result of a harmonious adjustment of the inner with the outer, of the man with his surroundings.

A man only begins to be a man when he ceases to whine and revile, and commences to search for the hidden justice which regulates his life. And as he adapts his mind to that regulating factor, he ceases to accuse others as the cause of his condition, and builds himself up in strong and noble thoughts; ceases to kick against circumstances, but begins to use them as aids to his more rapid progress, and as a means of discovering the hidden powers and possibilities within himself.

Law, not confusion, is the dominating principle in the universe; justice, not injustice, is the soul and substance of life; and righteousness, not corruption, is the moulding and moving force in the spiritual government of the world. This being so, man has but to right himself to find that the universe is right; and during the process of putting himself right he will find that as he alters his thoughts towards things and other people, things and other people will alter towards him.

The proof of this truth is in every person, and it therefore admits of easy investigation by systematic introspection and self-analysis. Let a man radically alter his thoughts, and he will be astonished at the rapid transformation it will effect in the material conditions of his life. Men imagine that thought can be kept secret, but it cannot; it rapidly crystallizes into habit, and habit solidifies into circumstance. Bestial thoughts crystallize into habits of drunkenness and sensuality, which solidify into circumstances of destitution and disease: impure thoughts of every kind crystallize into enervating and confusing habits, which solidify into distracting and adverse circumstances: thoughts of fear, doubt, and indecision crystallize into weak, unmanly, and irresolute habits, which solidify into circumstances of failure, indigence, and slavish dependence: lazy thoughts crystallize into habits of uncleanliness and dishonesty, which solidify into circumstances of foulness and beggary: hateful and condemnatory thoughts crystallize into habits of accusation and violence, which solidify into circumstances of injury and persecution: selfish thoughts of all kinds crystallize into habits of self-seeking, which solidify into circumstances more or less distressing. On the other hand, beautiful thoughts of all kinds crystallize into habits of grace and kindliness, which solidify into genial and sunny circumstances: pure thoughts crystallize into habits of temperance and self-control, which solidify into circumstances of repose and peace: thoughts of courage, self-reliance, and decision crystallize into manly habits, which solidify into circumstances of success, plenty, and freedom: energetic thoughts crystallize into habits of cleanliness and industry, which solidify into circumstances of pleasantness: gentle and forgiving thoughts crystallize into habits of gentleness, which solidify into protective and preservative circumstances: loving and unselfish thoughts crystallize into habits of self-forgetfulness for others, which solidify into circumstances of sure and abiding prosperity and true riches.

A particular train of thought persisted in, be it good or bad, cannot fail to produce its results on the character and circumstances. A man cannot directly choose his circumstances, but he can choose his thoughts, and so indirectly, yet surely, shape his circumstances.

Nature helps every man to the gratification of the thoughts, which he most encourages, and opportunities are presented which will most speedily bring to the surface both the good and evil thoughts.

Let a man cease from his sinful thoughts, and all the world will soften towards him, and be ready to help him; let him put away his weakly and sickly thoughts, and lo, opportunities will spring up on every hand to aid his strong resolves; let him encourage good thoughts, and no hard fate shall bind him down to wretchedness and shame. The world is your kaleidoscope, and the varying combinations of colours, which at every succeeding moment it presents to you are the exquisitely adjusted pictures of your ever-moving thoughts.

So
You will be what you will to be;
Let failure find its false content
In that poor word, 'environment,'
But spirit scorns it, and is free.
'It masters time, it conquers space;
It cowes that boastful trickster, Chance,
And bids the tyrant Circumstance
Uncrown, and fill a servant's place.
'The human Will, that force unseen,
The offspring of a deathless Soul,
Can hew a way to any goal,
Though walls of granite intervene.
'Be not impatient in delays
But wait as one who understands;
When spirit rises and commands
The gods are ready to obey.

EFFECT OF THOUGHT ON HEALTH AND THE BODY

The body is the servant of the mind. It obeys the operations of the mind, whether they be deliberately chosen or automatically expressed. At the bidding of unlawful thoughts the body sinks rapidly into disease and decay; at the command of glad and beautiful thoughts it becomes clothed with youthfulness and beauty.

Disease and health, like circumstances, are rooted in thought. Sickly thoughts will express themselves through a sickly body. Thoughts of fear have been known to kill a man as speedily as a bullet, and they are continually killing thousands of people just as surely though less rapidly. The people who live in fear of disease are the people who get it. Anxiety quickly demoralizes the whole body, and lays it open to the entrance of disease; while impure thoughts, even if not physically indulged, will soon shatter the nervous system.

Strong, pure, and happy thoughts build up the body in vigour and grace. The body is a delicate and plastic instrument, which responds readily to the thoughts by which it is impressed, and habits of thought will produce their own effects, good or bad, upon it.

Men will continue to have impure and poisoned blood, so long as they propagate unclean thoughts. Out of a clean heart comes a clean life and a clean body. Out of a defiled mind proceeds a defiled life and a corrupt body. Thought is the fount of action, life, and manifestation; make the fountain pure, and all will be pure.

Change of diet will not help a man who will not change his thoughts. When a man makes his thoughts pure, he no longer desires impure food. Clean thoughts make clean habits. The so-called saint who does not wash his body is not a saint. He who has strengthened and purified his thoughts does not need to consider the malevolent microbe.

If you would protect your body, guard your mind. If you would renew your body, beautify your mind. Thoughts of malice, envy, disappointment, despondency, rob the body of its health and grace. A sour face does not come by chance; it is made by sour thoughts. Wrinkles that mar are drawn by folly, passion, and pride.

I know a woman of ninety-six who has the bright, innocent face of a girl. I know a man well under middle age whose face is drawn into inharmonious contours. The one is the result of a sweet and sunny disposition; the other is the outcome of passion and discontent.

As you cannot have a sweet and wholesome abode unless you admit the air and sunshine freely into your rooms, so a strong body and a bright, happy, or serene countenance can only result from the free admittance into the mind of thoughts of joy and goodwill and serenity.

On the faces of the aged there are wrinkles made by sympathy, others by strong and pure thought, and others are carved by passion: who cannot distinguish them? With those who have lived righteously, age is calm, peaceful, and softly mellowed, like the setting sun. I have recently seen a philosopher on his deathbed. He was not old except in years. He died as sweetly and peacefully as he had lived.

There is no physician like cheerful thought for dissipating the ills of the body; there is no comforter to compare with goodwill for dispersing the shadows of grief and sorrow. To live continually in thoughts of ill will, cynicism, suspicion, and envy, is to be confined in a self made prison-hole. But to think well of all, to be cheerful with all, to patiently learn to find the good in all—such unselfish thoughts are the very portals of heaven; and to dwell day by day in thoughts of peace toward every creature will bring abounding peace to their possessor.

Acknowledgements

Excerpts from *The Success Sutra* by Devdutt Pattanaik are reprinted with the permission of the author.

'Why Leaders Should Be Mindful, Selfless, and Compassionate' and 'Countering Stress and Depression' by His Holiness the Dalai Lama are printed with permission from the Office of His Holiness the Dalai Lama.

Notes on the Contributors

Dale Carnegie was an American author and lecturer. He was born in poverty in Missouri in 1888. A skilful orator from a young age, Carnegie was active in his school debate team. He won several intercollegiate public speaking contests. He started his career as a salesman upon graduating from college in 1908. Following a brief stint as an actor in 1911, he taught his first public speaking course at the YMCA in New York. His courses soon became immensely popular and, by 1930, he began recruiting individuals to deliver courses in professional improvement throughout the country. He is considered a pioneer in self-improvement and his works including *How to Win Friends and Influence People* (1936) and *How to Stop Worrying and Start Living* (1948) are popular to this day. He died in 1955.

Devdutt Pattanaik writes, illustrates, and lectures on the relevance of mythology in modern times. He has, since 1996, written over fifty books and 1,000 columns on how stories, symbols, and rituals construct the subjective truth (myths) of ancient and modern cultures around the world. His books include *Pilgrim Nation, Business Sutra: A Very Indian Approach to Management, The Success Sutra: An Indian Approach to Wealth, The Talent Sutra: An Indian Approach to Learning*, and *The Leadership Sutra: An Indian Approach to Power.*

George Samuel Clason was an American author and businessman. He was born in Louisiana in 1874. He established the Clason Map Company in Colorado as well as the Clason Publishing Company. In the 1920s, he began writing pamphlets offering financial advice. Set in Babylon, these pamphlets were hugely popular with banks and insurance companies, and were compiled into *The Richest Man in Babylon*—a celebrated classic that has remained in print for a century. He died in California in 1957.

His Holiness, the 14th Dalai Lama, Tenzin Gyatso was born is north-eastern Tibet in 1935. He is the highest spiritual leader of Tibet. He also served as the political leader of Tibet before the democratization of the Tibetan administration. He is an advocate for world peace, interfaith harmony, and environmental reform. He has authored more than hundred books and is globally recognized for his teachings. He received the Nobel Peace Prize in 1989 and the US Congressional Gold Medal in 2006.

James Allen was born in 1864 to a working-class family in Leicester, England. Following the death of his father, he was forced to find work to support his family at the age of fifteen. Throughout the 1890s he worked as a secretary in a British manufacturing firm and later found a role in journalism. In 1898, he explored his interest in spirituality by writing for a magazine called the Herald of the Golden Age, and by 1902, he started his own publication called *The Epoch*. After retiring in 1903, he lived in a small town in North Devon with his wife, Lily, and daughter, Nora, and continued writing until his death in 1912. *As a Man Thinketh*, published in 1903, is his third and most famous work.

Joseph Murphy was born in Ireland in 1898. He joined the Jesuits at an early age and began preparing to be initiated into the priesthood. However, he then decided to emigrate to America and became a pharmacist in New York City. He was interested in the study of different religions and travelled to India to learn about Asian religions. He later started his own church in Los Angeles in the 1940s. He earned a PhD in psychology from the University of South California and wrote thirty books in the self-help genre. *The Power of Your Subconscious Mind*, which was published in 1963, is his most famous work. Murphy died in 1981.

Napoleon Hill was an American motivational author. He was born in Virginia in 1883 and started writing at the age of thirteen. He is most famous for his work *Think and Grow Rich*, an all-time bestseller published in 1937. He established the Napoleon Hill Foundation, a non-profit institution that promotes his philosophy of personal achievement, leadership, and success. He died in 1970.

Paramhansa Yogananda was a guru, yogi, and writer from Gorakhpur, Uttar Pradesh. He is credited with introducing Kriya Yoga to a global audience. His book *Autobiography of a Yogi*, published in 1946, met with critical and commercial success. He died in Los Angeles in 1952.